Skylantern Dragons and the Monsters of Mundor

Scott W. Taylor

A Tailored Toons Paperback

*All characters in this publication are fictitious
and any resemblance to real persons, living or
dead, is purely coincidental.*

All rights reserved. No part of this publication may be reproduced, stored in a retrieval system, or transmitted, in any form or by any means, without the prior permission in writing of the publisher, nor be otherwise circulated in any form of binding or cover other than that in which it is published and without a similar condition including this condition being imposed on the subsequent purchaser.

*All characters in this book were created by
and are owned by Tailored Toons.
Find Tailoredtoons on Facebook and Instagram.*

*http://m.facebook.com/Ravenskarr/
or http//www.tailoredtoonspublishing.co.uk*

ISBN 978-1-5272-3048-4

Printed and bound in Great Britain
by Clays Ltd, Elcograf S.p.A.

THIS BOOK IS DEDICATED TO

Jane and Barry Taylor without whom this endeavour would never have existed.

Also

I would like to thank Adrian and Mandy Wheelhouse for their continued help and advice.

and

Stephen Blanchard for his time and attention to detail whilst editing this book.

and

Chris Matsell for his advice on social media marketing.

CONTENTS

PROEM	8
Chapter 1	11
Chapter 2	19
Chapter 3	35
Chapter 4	66
Chapter 5	85
Chapter 6	107
Chapter 7	118
Chapter 8	127
Chapter 9	138
Chapter 10	163
Chapter 11	208
Chapter 12	227
Chapter 13	253
Chapter 14	275

"Let me be, was all I wanted. Be what I am, no matter how I am."

Henry Miller, *Stand Still Like the Hummingbird*

"The most important kind of freedom is to be what you really are. You trade in your reality for a role. You trade in your sense for an act. You give up your ability to feel, and in exchange, put on a mask."

Jim Morrison

PROEM

In all the backward worlds there are still taboos. Hence mistakes are committed, leaving in its wake a dwindling trust, increasing anger and ruin.

The only reason things go wrong to start with is that some people are unwilling to see the dark truths that dwell in the heart, and are less inclined to speak of them.

Love too maybe forbidden, for it carries the seed of violation, bringing consequence to all involved.

But what if I were to tell you, dear reader, that not all taboos border on the carnal, or the preferences of gender?

I shall tell the story of an unlikely thing.

Let me enlighten you of the alchemy of man. For such a price carries a stigma. Like lycanthropy where during a full moon a seemingly harmless individual can fall prey to the inner beast.

But let me say that it is quite possible for a man to become other creatures, beasts of myth and legend for example.

Instantly such things become paradigms and are soon whispered as curses.

For the misjudged heart of man soon learns the harsh realities of silence and loneliness. And they pray for the day that someone wise and sympathetic will, out of love and understanding, show them the path to happiness.

A way out of darkness.

Chapter 1

Mundor was a high, weather-beaten citadel. This realm was stark with the silhouettes of trees, damp, and austere without leaves, without the promise of a spring to come. It was home to a king who knew sorrow like the gravity and weight of duty, and felt his back arc and bend beneath its crude burden.

It was mid evening by the time King René called the council together for a meeting.

Behind him, hung like bunting from the bleak stone wall, was the crest of his house—a ruby red dragon burning the heart and sceptre of men, a harsh reminder of a past long diminished. There was a grave look about the man's weathered, bearded features as he began to voice his concerns, addressing his advisers from across the great wooden table.

'The day we all feared has come. The Sinistrom have approached our borders.'

The level of sounds rose as mutterings among the gathering increased; they all felt trepidation at this news.

'But,' he went on, cutting through the buzz suddenly, 'I have devised a plan which should buy us some time at least.'

There was a silence. A heavy question mark filled the hush, one which King René was only too pleased to break with an explanation.

'I have sent word to the Sinistrom that we wish to talk terms of peace.'

The mutterings erupted again.

'They are sending us a representative, someone with whom we can talk directly and convey our sincerity.'

'This is madness!' spoke out a member of the court, his grey hair hanging about his face. 'The Sinistrom will never listen to a plea of reconciliation, not in a thousand years!'

'They will listen.' The king asserted. 'They are sending us an ambassador. Their armies are too great. We would not last a day if it came to all out war. Peace is our only hope, gentlemen.'

King René could tell from just looking at all the faces that many of his people were skeptical, though the king's word was law and whatever he decided must ultimately be accepted.

Once the king dismissed the council, René called for his son. A nearby servant shrugged.

'No one has seen the prince, sire,' the servant answered boldly.

'What do you mean "no one has seen him?"' the king bellowed.

'He left this morning, sire. He told no one where he was going. He simply left without any explanation.'

The king rubbed his temple. This was not the first time the prince had wandered off without a word. This vexed René.

A storm front approached, filling the skies with darkened cloud, and an oppressive wind brought many of the trees in the royal courts toppling to the ground. But this was nothing compared to the truly appalling situation that had arisen, though King René was prepared to meet it head on.

Thousands of Sinistrom soldiers, Mecha Villeforms, stood in regimented formations before the armies of King René. The light infantry at the head of the apposing army were cybernetic creatures, humanoid, part metal, but mostly maggot. They were foul, unctuous creatures with white, slime covered skin, and equipped with technologically advanced armaments. They had wide necks with large compound eyes and crushing beaks. Some rode on caterpillars the size of horses and held the banners of their king, the mighty Kardas Vallor. In addition, holding fast behind those front lines, were many other breeds and types, all allied together: Harpies, Centaurs, Hydras, Minotaur, even humans. There were Gorgons and Medusas, as well as creatures that had borne no mention in prior tales. Snakes, vicious, scaly viper masters had traveled to fight alongside the Sinistrom armies. They had come from the dark citadel in the south. Among these snakes were the familiars known as Ohidia, a female warrior with pale green skin and tall, slender frame. And Tai Pan, the shape shifter and trickster. There was Sawscale, the viper with his armory of buzz saws and knives. Hooknose with his mighty tusks that protruded from his head like spears. The others, Coach Whip with his tri corner hat, Black Monda, and Cotton Jaw, proved a formidable presence. But none of these foul fusiliers compared to the dark and terrible Malecarjan. This tall figure with menacing proportions sat astride his coal-black steed. His face was a mystery forever, concealed behind a plumed helmet, his eyes glowing bright red behind a dark void and an iron grate.

Standing next to Malecarjan was a man who was rather smartly dressed, though his choice of threads perhaps were more in keeping with someone wishing to close a business deal and set a good example, rather than participate in bloody hostilities. He was the true enigma in this immense gathering. He looked to be a gentleman in his 50s with a mane of white hair, a stoic appearance, and eyes that were black as pitch, with red dilated pupils.

The two opposing armies faced each other, one clearly outnumbered by the other. King René looked on and was in awe. There was no chance in hell of winning in an all out confrontation with such numbers as these. The only option was diplomacy. Why diplomacy? Why did he believe negotiation was viable? Because he saw hope with the one stranger who seemed out of place among the hordes of the Sinistrom army. He saw optimism when he witnessed the black eyed man standing there. This man was definitely in a position of authority.

Biting the bullet, King René rode out to meet his enemy on horseback. Malecarjan's stallion grunted and panted, exhibiting a growing restlessness. Its master reached forward with an iron glove and gave the side of its head a gentle pat. Finally, his hand stayed at the sword sheathed at his side.

Black eyes put up his hands, knowing the rash and belligerent nature of his general, and indicated to Malecarjan to stand down.

'Make no sudden moves!' His grip tightened on his katana hilt.

René slowed as he approached the enigma. The stranger was indeed foreign to these parts. His features were like nothing he had seen. And those eyes were the devil's. Nevertheless, he seemed to exude an air of trust.

Dismounting from his horse, King René continued to approach the man on foot. The enigma stepped forward, the two men meeting face to face.

'I admire your courage and your wisdom.' The black eyed man saw the king in the highest regard. 'These traits are regarded as high commodities among the Sinistrom.'

Silently, Malecarjan turned his head away as he did not share his master's views.

'I'm here to discuss a peaceful alternative to war,' said the king. The potentate was holding himself tall, falling upon his experience as a diplomat, and constantly mindful of his posture, his attitude; knowing to speak clearly, even though he was anxious. He had no intention of revealing that he was.

The enigma smiled. Those black eyes with two tiny red points at their core were like razorblades, fixed upon a point, and probing. He had once thought the native peoples of this realm were barbaric and thuggish. It was nice to be proven wrong once in a while.

'I am glad to hear it,' the enigma replied, frankly. 'Under our borders we would enjoy many years of trade, and you would prosper greatly under Sinistrom protection. I am John by the way—John Dafoe!'

The black eyed individual took the king's hand, agreeing to cease fire, and allow talks to begin.

René allowed himself a moment of curiosity. He had witnessed the sword at John's side, and felt that its size and dimensions, not to mention its ornate decorativeness, added a certain grace, and a more refined edge. It was a lot smaller and lighter in appearance than the common broad swords that were wielded by his soldiers. John Dafoe recognised this unique opportunity to show his potential ally the weapon.

'It is called a Katana,' the man said, lifting the strap that held the sheath over his head. He handed the king the sword which was more a piece of art than a weapon. 'On my world, the world where we originated, it was a formidable weapon. Lightweight, it was forged by the artist's hand, its steel melted, and folded many times over to give it precise sharpness.'

'It is beautiful and such masterful craftsmanship.'

The king offered a humbled smile.

'It puts our own swords to shame.' He added, handing the weapon back to its keeper respectfully.

The king tightened his lips as though prompted to convey a rather bold idea. This required much confidence, and throwing caution to the wind finally he made his invitation.

'We are holding a banquet. You and your dignitaries are quite welcome to join us if you like. We have wine from the provinces, venison, good music, and entertainments. You will be our guests of honour.'

John smiled as he placed his sword at his side.

'That is very thoughtful, my friend. We thank you, and may I say on behalf of all the Sinistrom that we would be thrilled and flattered to accept your gracious invitation.'

'Tonight, then? Evenfall.'

The enigma lowered his black eyes in response, and then turned to rejoin his army.

King René did the same. He gave a deep breath as he walked away, filling his uneasy lungs, giving them a chance to overcome the highly sensitive task he had just undertaken, and knowing that it wasn't quite over yet.

Chapter 2

Prince Fabian stood completely still in the deep forest, trying to take stock of his motives for being in this savage place. This was the farthest he had ever wandered. Before, necessity had always forced him to turn back to what was safe and recognisable. He just didn't have the guts to venture out any further, or so he kept telling himself. But then, there was something so compelling about the unknown. And there was something deep within him, something missing, something that haunted him, passionate and suffocating, dogging his every need. There was indeed another life beyond the known, another existence. There was indeed a bigger world if only he had the nerve to chase it.

That provincial life had conjured more questions than answers. Here amidst the trees and the lonely silence he felt one question repeating in his mind:

What was he doing here?

What reason did he have to come all this way and risk the unknown? Was it for the quiet? Was it for the solitude? No. He could experience loneliness at the castle where duty and old-fashioned beliefs and customs waited for him. Why then? There was only one answer. He had stirrings more primal than he cared to admit. It was as if another being, another entity was inside him, clawing to get out.

Through the silence he heard a faint cry. Snapping his head in the direction of the distant sound, he moved, fleet of foot.

Dashing between the trees, Fabian stumbled out into a clearing.

'Ahhh,' came the cry again. He charged back into the trees, moving as fast as he could through the tripping roots and dense underbrush that grew this deep in the forest. The sweet, enticing smell of aloe struck his nose as he got closer to the calls for help: the cruel stench of a predator. He broke the tree line into an open valley where a young boy lay, wrapped in the thick green vines of a giant pitcher plant. The human boy was being dragged slowly toward the gaping maw. Mucus frothed and bubbled over razor sharp teeth that dripped with aloe.

Without once thinking of his own safety, Prince Fabian drew his dagger and went to save the boy. He wasn't fast enough. Another slimy tentacle snapped outward, catching the prince by the ankle. With a sharp howl the prince was brought off balance. He was quickly on his back, being hauled along in the dirt. All he had done was doom himself as he watched the tiny child next to him being dragged towards his death. With the blade in his hand Fabian found it difficult to cut the vines around his ankles since he was in a rather clumsy position. Instead he attempted to thrust the blade into the ground to allow him some grip. He noticed the mouth with its dripping enzymes. There were bones mixed with the foul froth and mucus acids. These bones were stripped of their flesh. Some other animal had strayed too close for comfort and had suffered slowly as the acids had consumed it.

The boy's screams were deafening at this point. He tried grasping on to stones, grass, turf, anything that appeared rooted, but further he went, advancing towards the mouth that would strip him of his flesh.

Prince Fabian could not have predicted what happened next, since it had only occurred once when he was very young, and only partially. He suddenly recognised it, the impulsive feeling of rage and power. The transformation. A metamorphosis of man into dragon!

Holding on to a tree root, he noticed the sudden

discoloration on his hands, the odd rose-colored tincture, and the veins and capillaries of his flesh grew in size. All up his arm this strange phenomenon began to spread. His veins turned black and were almost like small pipes beneath his throbbing tissue. His fingers were extending outwards, becoming more feral in appearance, and less like human appendages. How fortunate that the young boy was unaware of this as his eyes were transfixed by the plant's mouth, chomping and grinding with eagerness for the kill. That poor child. It would have been unforgivably wicked to have added to the victim's terror, particularly as he was already driven out of his wits by the panic that held him.

The world and all its colours were washed away, replaced by the red tint of passion in Fabian's eyes. He felt his muscles enlarging beneath his leather tunic. His clawed hands had grown and distended beyond the size and stature of any mortal hands. He could no longer speak or utter words, but he could emit certain low grunts, feeling much of his higher brain functions slip away. He only understood the primal needs of his nature. And the power and the anger grew fiercely behind his blood-red eyes.

In Prince Fabian's place there stood a great crimson dragon. It raised its horned head proudly, elevating its arms, slowly and with poise. The large ruby muscles and sinews rippled beneath the covering of scales. The great reptile situated itself on two hind legs. It was at least 14 feet in height. Humanoid in shape, the dragon basked in the clearing, resembling a majestic beast that had found its freedom of expression. Its wings, webbed and elongated, unfurled like bright red sepals. It inhaled vast amounts of air, filling its mighty lungs to capacity, and then, forcing that air out through the nostrils, ignited momentary plumes of fire. The vines of the killer plant were still tangled round its legs. The dragon gave a cocky and conceited smile. Grasping onto the tendrils and vines, it began to tug at the plant. The great vegetable rasped and shrieked as it soon discovered it was rudely outmatched. It was quickly uprooted, yanked from the very earth that had been its territory for so long. The child was released quickly from the vine's clutches. Taking hold of the rest of the vines, the dragon creature used its immense strength to swing the monstrous maw above its head, pitching it in all directions before eventually letting go. The gaping maw and all its flailing vines catapulted high into the trees and was impaled upon the thorny brushwood.

The little boy sat stock still with scrapes and bruises all over his legs and up his arms. He was terrified even to move. This strange dragon-creature had suddenly appeared to save his life, though for what despicable purpose he could not tell. Perhaps the dragon was a fiercer predator, its elongated face and nose hiding those razor-sharp teeth, and its ruby red chin that glistened with saliva. The eyes seemed momentarily inflamed as they met with the boy's troubled gaze, but the dragon merely stood there. It was as if it didn't know what to do next. The webbed wings behind its back slowly dropped and folded away. Its red eyes did not appear to engender the presence of evil, but contrition. Then, out of disgust or penitence, it disappeared into the thicket with a single bound. The threat was gone. Or so it appeared. The child began to cry out, filling the forest with an appeal, a desperate call for his father.

At the border of the forest Prince Fabian lay unconscious for a short time. He dreamed of the shining red dragon, a power beyond his control, a hatred stimulated by anger and rage. He woke suddenly, feeling the sun on his back, the heat on his bare flesh. It didn't take him long to realise he was naked. Silence merged with confusion as the prince looked down at his hands. A few minor lacerations had appeared, though he had no memory of anything after his transformation. He heard a gunshot in the distance. Somewhere a flock of crows took to the skies, filling the air with their beating wings and cries.

'Get up! Get up I say!'

The voice was full of disgust and anger.

Prince Fabian's vision had not yet fully cleared. He could make out the vague shape of a man and he could feel the rough sensation of a padded glove on his arm, gripping tightly, urging him to stand.

Vision slowly began to return. Soon he realised he was being addressed by two of the king's men. They had come to take him back. This was far from good news. Soon he was escorted home, draped in a long flowing gown, and wearing a cowl to conceal his identity from all onlookers as they neared the castle boundaries. By this time he could feel the shame of his father, the embarrassment of the captain of the guard who had already seen him, and the silent mocking of those who served under him. This saddened and angered the young prince. It saddened him because he was being hauled back in such disgrace and angered because no one trusted him, or accepted him for who he was. He had left this place to find something, but all he had found was this prison of fear he had known all his life. He could not escape the incarceration that not only enslaved him daily, but jeered at his differences, and beat him down for his apparent improprieties. He could not have felt more alone, surrounded as he was by all these boorish countrymen. Disconsolate, spirit crushed, and impotent to rebel, he planned his escape…where? Where could he go that did not fill every fiber of his being with terror? Or journey that did not bring him crawling back to the common and familiar hell he had known all his life? He hated his own timidity and felt abashed at his helplessness and lack of courage. For there was one thing he feared more than the unknown, and that was facing his father's irritation.

'Your Father will see you now,' the captain of the guard said, making it sound more like a begrudged command than a humble request. The door to the royal chambers was opened and this shabby object of ridicule, dressed in a robe and cowl, was ushered in.

'What have you to say for yourself?' uttered the deep and commanding voice.

Prince Fabian could not bring himself to raise his head to look at the man sitting upon the ancient throne.

'Explain!' the grizzled, old potentate barked at him.

The boy didn't answer, could not answer. Silence was his solitary response. However, the words of his father did not stave the plotting of his mind, did not prevent the chattering of his thoughts, or the words he did not dare utter out loud.

Before he knew what was happening, his father was on his feet. He strode up to him, tearing the cloak from his bare flesh, exposing his nakedness to the light. Prince Fabian could not have felt more inferior than he did at that moment.

'Cowering child! I wish I had left you for dead! One heir to the throne of Mundor and you had to embarrass me, in front of the guards…again! You spit in my face and make a mockery of all that we have built!'

The older man tightened his lips as he looked on in disgust at the boy standing before him.

'A pity your mother died.' He continued to speak upon reflection. He turned his back to tend the fire, jabbing the hot coals with a poker. The blaze rose and sparked as it offered a warm glow to the icy temperature of the room.

'Now I am left with you,' he stated finally, the disappointment evident in his voice.

It was at that moment the son and heir decided to speak up.

'I have known a mother's love. Once…before the accident…'

His voice cracked with emotion. He looked at his father whose back was turned to him in loathing.

'My mother always spoke to me with kindness, told me of the days when men lived with more optimism than they do now.'

His voice sounded weak and inoffensive because, even though he felt angry, he did not wish to provoke his father's rage any more than he had to.

'Men?' The old man echoed the boy's words. 'You speak of men, though you have no idea what it is to be a man.'

Propping the poker against the fireplace, the king turned to view his son with an accusing look in his beady, little eyes.

'I have never met anyone quite like you. You are abhorrent to me, something alien, a crude malformation that will one day sit upon this throne. And on that day, Mundor will witness not a king, but a fool. A cretin whose weakness will be an invitation to our enemies! On that day Mundor will fall to ruin. No, I have never met anyone quite like you.'

'My mother raised me to be an individual, that which you find so sickening. She taught me to cherish independence, and to acknowledge an era when these traits were commonplace and accepted.'

'I do not care! You hear me? You are a prince of the realm and mark my words, boy, you will damn well act like one.'

The king's voice was low and rasping. The boy could not bear to hear his mother's values played down in such a fashion.

'You dare, father.' Fabian's words were nothing more than a weakling whine.

The king's eyes narrowed, twitching with rage.

'Get out.'

The boy looked astonished.

The older man turned on his heels, brandishing the metal poker which he snatched from the wall.

'Get out!'

The boy feared that this time his father was going to beat him within an inch of his life. Quickly he bent down to grabbed the gown from the floor and darted from the king's chambers, the long robe tethered to his midriff like a towel.

He knew the extent of his father's rage. After all, Fabian was the only one present when his mother had her throat torn out. He watched her blood spill, staining the virgin snow. René blamed his son for not taking swift and stern action against a fanged killer as it bore down on the defenseless parent. His mother was killed, and Fabian did nothing but cower and cry. Time and time again Fabian tried to explain to his father that that prince who sat on horseback, wailing and whimpering, was but a child. The creature that carried away his mother was a fiend, larger than life, and more terrifying than anything he had seen. But still, his father did not believe a word of it.

The king stood alone, muttering in his chambers, erecting barriers in all directions, and fuelling the estrangement of his son. How in God's name could he even hope to bridge the gap between Mundor and the hordes of the Sinistrom when he didn't even love his own wayward son? Two conflicting emotions rose to beat him down at every turn. How could he reconcile such a paradox? How could he talk peace if peace itself eluded him?

The King settled in his seat. Looking up from his musings, he cast his eyes finally to the large chamber door, slightly ajar, and noticed the small shape standing there.

'Been eavesdropping again, dwarf!'

The short little man noticed suddenly that his presence had been detected and, not wanting to incur the king's anger, backed slowly and stealthily into the shadows.

The king shot to his feet angrily.

'Dirty tunnel Dweller! That's it, scurry back to your hovel!'

Prince Fabian was back in his room. He was not seen for what seemed like hours. The young heir stared at his reflection in the mirror, looking deep into his likeness, wondering what monster had revealed itself in the woods that day. He looked pale and, in truth he was concerned that it would happen again, this terrible metamorphosis. All he remembered from the events earlier that day was the feeling that something else, something terrifying was trapped within his flesh, clawing to come out. He recalled how his skin became discoloured, and the appalling way in which his bones reshaped themselves, as if, by means of enchantment, he was becoming someone or something else entirely. A cold sweat covered his brow. He grasped his hand quickly to stop it from shaking.

There was a knock at the door. He wasn't expecting visitors. He couldn't allow himself to be seen so agitated and upset. Wiping his hand across his brow, he called out:

'Who is it?'

'It's only I,' uttered a familiar voice.

This was not the time for visitors, Prince Fabian mused. Neither was it the appropriate time for raising suspicions. But Fabian knew the voice belonged to Tweak, the local busybody and alchemist.

'Come!' he shouted.

The door opened and in trod a dwarf with the most curious features. Thick brown hair framed his face, and the bushiest brows flanked a pair of odd looking spectacles that sat upon the bridge of a rather pronounced, generously sized nose. The spectacles gave one the impression of an antique watch design, making the dwarf appear as if he was a tinker of a sort, capable of dabbling in the most rudimentary of sciences. But what was even more curious was the fact that he had not two, but four ears that jutted outwards from his mane of thick hair. This dwarf had the ears of an ass, long and tall, and perfect for eavesdropping.

'Why the long face?' Tweak asked.

Prince Fabian was hardly in the mood for a social call, but he tried to hide his true emotions, if only to delay any misgivings.

'No. You just startled me, that's all.'

'Hope I'm not intruding.'

'No, not at all,' he lied.

Prince Fabian looked again at his reflection for one

fleeting moment, and suddenly he caught something dark and twisted gazing back at him. It was a second, but there was something that undeniably caught his eye: a dragon's reflection.

'Now I know something is wrong.' Tweak deduced.

'Well, I am not at liberty to tell you anything at the moment, Tweak. I'm sorry. Now if you don't mind I would like to be alone. Please respect my wishes, my old friend. I – I don't want to talk about it.'

Silently, the dwarf stepped away, shutting the door behind him. Something was terribly wrong and it was up to this resident busy-body to find out just what. Far be it for old 'eavesdropper' Tweak, as he was referred to by most around the court, to stand idly by when there was gossip to be uncovered, as well as a hidden crisis to be exposed.

Tweak shuffled back to his lodgings. Opening the door, he loosened a collection of mystic contrivances, broomsticks, flying carpets, wooden steps, which slid down past the door frame, making a loud clatter as they hit the pebbled floor. He gurned in his habitual manner, shrugged and swiftly moved towards his bookshelves. There had to be a tome, some specific manuscript, in his collection containing a magic spell that would help loosen the Prince's tongue. But then a case of wine would likely provide the same results. No, such crude methods were not the answer.

Shortly, the answer came to him. He would use the mirror of secrets to discover what Prince Fabian was hiding. True, he thought to himself, the use of such a powerful looking glass was an impropriety, but then, desperate times called for desperate actions. Uncovering his mirror, he began to whisper a short mantra before his reflection. Soon the manifestation of his likeness changed to be replaced by the image of trees. There was a child who had been snared by a carnivorous plant. Fear was evident on the boy's face as the vines coiled around his legs. Tweak witnessed as Prince Fabian entered the fray, getting captured as well.

A look of surprise came over Tweak's face. What transpired brought a whole new dimension to the horror. Tweak backed away from the reflection in the glass as it presented the past in its entirety. Tweak witnessed an unexpected transformation. The eyes of the dwarf grew wider as the full revelation began to unravel.

The Prince! He's a dragon!

Chapter 3

The great banquet hall was alive with talk as the three guests of honour entered. General Dafoe was the first to be announced, along with his Lieutenant, Malecarjan, followed by a curious and attractive man who looked to be round the age of 16. This was Tør. He was the ambassador, the one who would conduct the talks. This man was also the proud beneficiary to the great empire which he represented and son to the great king Kardas Vallor.

Tør was the first person who captured the Prince's eye as he entered the great banquet hall. There was that unmistakable sensation of attraction, a feeling the young heir had rarely experienced in the past. There was a moment when their eyes met. The ambassador who appeared to be a couple of years younger than Prince Fabian, had such beautiful and captivating features. Seemingly his charms were not only noticed by Fabian as there was a considerable aggregate of young women present, both of nobility as well as those who were in the employ of the court. They clustered together and watched, taking in the appearance of his long, dark, curly hair and chestnut complexion, as well as those chiseled features and high cheekbones. Though his eyes were indeed the loveliest facets of them all, accentuated by the longest lashes Fabian had seen on a man. The ambassador was particularly well groomed and, like the strange enigma who accompanied him, indulged in a fashion alien to this realm.

Each of the three representatives was ushered to their seats. Dafoe smiled and nodded affably and respectfully to the other guests. He was dressed elegantly in a plush, black shirt and trousers, matching perfectly the tincture of his eyes. Malecarjan stood behind him and was consistently silent, unspoken as the grave. He had made no effort to change and appeared as if the very helmet he wore was welded permanently to his head. It gave one the impression that he had no wish to display his true face. That was the most sinister aspect. As Dafoe sat down at the table Malecarjan lingered and continued to stand, remaining a cold and baleful presence.

'Please be seated,' said the king at last, addressing the entire room. 'Let our feast commence. And let us raise a toast to our guests. May this banquet be the first evidence that we, our two respective houses can drink and share good food together.'

The potentate raised his goblet.

'To friendship!'

The room was alive with talk as those who were opposed to the possible treaty between these two armies had not attended. Only the unwitting were celebrating along with their king who, quite frankly, was willing to compromise all to quell that unstoppable force that was at his gate.

It took a little while before Fabian plucked up enough courage to ask one of the Ambassador's aides the name of the fetching young man in question. According to the assistant present his name was Tør. Tør Vallor!

Fabian was in a whirlwind of anticipation. Never had he seen such beauty, never in all his born years, though the slightest desire on his part would have proven inappropriate, especially since the object of his yearning was another man.

It was then when he noticed the Ambassador leaving the room via the large open veranda. Bravely, Fabian began to follow.

The prince stepped outside into the veranda. He witnessed the shadow of his desire pass through the garden beyond, entering the arboretum by a portico camouflaged by a canopy of vines.

Making his way down the steps and then sprinting across the lawn in the dead of night, Fabian attempted to catch up with the young ambassador. When he finally discovered him, the ambassador was standing alone with his back turned. The prince took a few silent steps closer, stopping at the ambassador's side. The younger man noticed his presence and looked at Fabian, smiling.

'Those moons of Mundor.' Tør mentioned. 'They are both impressively beautiful.'

Fabian did not let on that he was nervous. He had watched the attractive young man, noticing his unwavering curiosity of the night sky.

The ambassador continued to watch the twin satellites, the smallest almost encompassed by the second.

'Where I came from…' Tør began to explain. 'There was but one light in the night sky…' And he turned, smiling. 'Not counting the stars of course.'

The prince stood his ground, feeling as nervous as hell.

The ambassador chose not to regard the prince's discomfort, knowing full well what power he wielded over others.

The young man turned to regard the heavenly bodies again, this time leaning upon a tree. The prince came alongside him. The gardens bordering the castle were indeed enchanting in the late hours, but not quite as captivating as those eyes. Eyes that peered at the moons with such dream-like reverence.

'It sounds as though you miss your home,' professed Fabian, trying to make conversation without appearing too intrusive.

The ambassador gave another smile, and only looked at his host for a second before returning his gaze to the celestial objects in the lucid sky.

'I was very young,' he admitted. 'What I do remember of my original home is from a recording, a simple holographic recording.'

'Excuse me?' the prince asked, unable to follow.

The ambassador had forgotten for only a moment that Mundor was a place of magic. Men here could only intuit a smattering of science, and only on a rudimentary level. It was available only to nobility. The weapons were muskets, and as such these primitive people had never heard of the wondrous and frightening technologies of other worlds. This sudden lapse of memory caused Tør to laugh inwardly at himself. Quickly, he removed a strange cube-like object from his coat pocket. It was small and metallic which had a curious sheen. It was like burnished obsidian.

'This,' Tør began to explain, 'is a holographic projection cube.'

The prince looked at the article in the other's hand, regarding it like a child that had never seen a piece of tech before.

'A hollow what?' he blurted out.

'A holographic projector,' Tør repeated. 'On my world it is as common as a broom handle. Here let me show you. You may want to close your eyes for a second.'

'Why?' the other asked.

'Because this cube emits a bright light which might be disorientating if you glimpse.'

Tør looked straight into Fabian's eyes. It was a steady, alluring gaze which made the other's heart race.

'Now close your eyes,' he said.

Not certain if this was some frivolous deception or hoax, Fabian was still reluctant to play along. Then he noted the miniature metal circle on top of the cube. It was like a key on a music box rotating fast at first, counter clockwise, and then slowing, visibly winding down. In spite of his doubts, he recognised his ignorance of technology and closed his eyes as he was told.

As the ambassador had warned, the holographic

cube emitted a blinding light that bathed the space around them, fusing darkness with a strange and palpable luminosity. The glow began to take a different shape, becoming something solid, or at least giving the appearance of solidity.

'You may open them now,' said the ambassador.

The moment Fabian opened his eyes he was astonished to see that his surroundings had altered dramatically. The arboretum was no longer in sight. The trees, the flowers, and the bushes, all with their strange and alluring topiary, had been replaced by rooms, dark rooms, with windows and art and strange architecture.

'Where are we?' he asked as his eyes darted from one wonder to the next. Fabian was understandably unsettled.

'We are still in the arboretum.' The ambassador assured him.

This did not assuage any of Fabian's fears or make him any less startled at this noticeable marvel.

'It is an enchantment!' he cried. 'This holo-whatever you call it is witchcraft! I demand you take me back to the grounds immediately!'

The ambassador thought his host's ingenuousness somewhat humorous, though had the good decency not to show it.

'Please, do not be afraid. This is no witchcraft, and it is definitely not magic. It is merely an illusion, and you are clearly not in any danger. This place,' he continued, casting his eyes along the long and lonely corridor, 'is where I grew up.'

Fabian was visibly in awe at the sight of this strange, alien environment.

'Then if this is not magic, what is it?'

'It would take far too long to explain,' responded the ambassador.

Fabian felt that Tør was indeed making sport of him. He cast him a look that implied that he was not in the least bit impressed.

'Are you telling me that it's beyond my comprehension?'

'For now, yes,' Tør answered. 'Though I do not share these marvels with you merely to show off. I did so because I sensed that you are an adventurous spirit. Perhaps you were in need of a revelation. You see, the Sinistrom want nothing more than to share what we know. To contribute, and to conquer, not with weapons or with words, but with ideas and sensations.

'On my world – this world you see around you – my father was a member of a movement called Mythkey. He and many others of our kind believed in a future world, a fair and sustainable world, a society based on wisdom rather than greed and injustice. We were not yet gods, and we were not yet fully aware of the sheer scope of our deeds and actions. We had spawned the most prevalent social interest group in human history. Though we did not realise the outcome of our goals, we strived nonetheless in changing human perceptions and making a better world for everyone. There had been many revolutions on our world, some had inevitably taken mankind in the wrong direction. And we, that is my forbears, had decided to put the course of human history back on the right track.'

Another side of the holographic cube suddenly came to life, emitting more images, illustrating the ambassador's narration with intricate shapes.

'But we could not save our world' he continued. 'It had spun completely out of control. We, the last remaining of our planet, now fade into the textbooks of history. You may look at us and think that we're gods, or devils, or powerful subjugators. But we are truly none of these things. Look at me. I am simply flesh and blood—like you. And like you we just want to coexist, to learn, and to teach. Trust me, Fabian; all I want is to share these memories with you now. These thoughts and feelings I have are meant to be shared. When you get to know us better you will find out that the Sinistrom only want to extend the knowledge. Knowledge we can both teach each other.

'When I first saw you I noticed at once that you were inquisitive, full of a fire that seeks answers.'

The prince felt his guard slowly weaken. He was starting to listen, as impressionable minds often did.

'I came from this very world. This was my home.' The ambassador went on to explain. 'Though it was beautiful, and full of marvels, it was also a place of falsehoods. Our gods who controlled our information did so in order so that they could misdirect people's attentions from what was actually going on.'

Fabian looked like a child in a huge candy store. The environment surrounding them – although a facsimile – seemed really strange. The wooden surfaces all arched like openings or doorways that led to spaces all filled with colour. Books on shelves fit side by side upon the walls and cold metal too, proudly sprung from one corner to the next, holding volumes and tomes, titles written in exotic tongues and modified with alien symbols. The crystalline tiaras that seemed to hang from the very ceiling, bunched together in attractive semicircles, provided light in no small way, acting much like candles. Such marvels as these were not to be missed or scoffed at. Beyond these spectacles even more were arrange. Areas were filled with such light it beggared belief. Everything aided in the flight of the imagination. Flat black and shiny surfaces sat like upright windows, adorning tables that defied logic. Fabian had no context upon which to draw any idea as to their function. Even the chairs had what looked like wheels on their legs.

'You said you used to live here. I still don't get what you mean by this. What exactly is "here"? This, whatever it is, is a world that did not exist until you used that strange cube object. It makes no sense.'

The ambassador started to rack his brains for some kind of example or the closest, basic analogy to illustrate what was unquestionably a failure to perceive a concept.

'Think of this as a tapestry,' he said finally. 'Like a tapestry woven by someone wishing to capture a moment in history—like a great battle! This you see all around you is nothing more than a refined tapestry that was woven to tell a story. Its many threads tell of a saga that once occurred on my own world a long, long time ago. I lived here, that is to say, I lived in a place that looked like this, in rooms just like these very rooms you see before you. But make no mistake, this you perceive is but a facsimile, a reproduction, a…a copy.'

'I think I see.' Fabian admitted a little hesitantly.

'This is the best way I can explain it to you. Some tapestries live on even after the original field of battle which they portrayed no longer exists. The same could be said for my home. It is the only living proof that my home existed. It lives on in the memory of my people and in this recording device.'

'You keep speaking of your world in the past tense. Does your home no longer exist?'

'You are quite correct,' answered the ambassador. 'My home was destroyed. It was destroyed, oh, a long time ago.'

'What destroyed it?' asked the prince.

'We were very foolish. We made mistakes. We believed in the power of gods and those same gods led us down a road of destruction.'

'Come on.' He gestured as he began to move away. 'I have something else to show you.'

Fabian followed. Or rather, he was finding it difficult to follow, but he was eager to learn more of the intricacies of Tør's world. He wanted to hear everything, know everything. He was being what he always dreamed of being. At last he was an explorer discovering many wondrous facets of distant lands. It was safe to say he was hooked. The ambassador, despite his youth, understood a lot about life and was surprisingly intelligent and well cultured for a man of his years.

'There,' Tør said, pointing, 'across the hallway. There you will discover another lesson in life, and perhaps the most pernicious lesson of all: regret.'

The ambassador pushed open another door. Here was a room, small and empty, dim and gloomy. Cobwebs dangled, suspended from the ceiling like wisps of paper. They moved lazily as the door emitted a draft. The only piece of furniture was an old wooden rocking chair with a small woven blanket draped over the seat. An odd looking box with moving pictures within its frame stood positioned next to a divider, where a thin slither of wallpaper had come away. Tør explained that the box was called a television set. Fabian was completely enthralled by the outwardly complex wonder of it. He would have enquired further to sate his curiosity, though Tør seemed to direct his attentions to the situation at hand.

'My grandfather's room.' Tør explained rather solemnly.

'Your grandfather lived here? In this great big building?'

'No. My grandfather died in a shabby tenement somewhere outside this city.'

Instantly, an elderly man appeared in the chair, materializing as a ghost, an apparition of a man whom had long remained dead. The facsimile rocked in that chair and coughed and spluttered like a man who was not long for this world.

The ambassador brazenly approached the old man. The holographic ghost in the chair didn't seem to notice the two intruders.

'Damn liars!' They both heard the old man curse.

A woman in her mid thirties with short mousy hair and a look of calm authority appeared as if suddenly conjured into existence and spoke to him.

'You whinging again?'

Fabian heard the voice which was feminine, firm, yet possessed a hint of playful wit. The prince pivoted round only to see a large woman barge passed, holding fresh sheets and a pillow. He snapped his hand to his chest, swearing blind that if anymore of these ghosts appeared his heart would probably stop.

The woman indicated to the old man to lean forwards so that she could place a fresh pillow behind his head. The old man rasped and coughed again. The television next to the wall was broadcasting some political debate.

'Yes, of course I'm whinging!' the old man snapped.

'You're always whinging.' She smiled in that annoying,

superior fashion which he hated and distrusted above all else.

'And what is wrong with that?' he asked. 'If people didn't whinge all the time nothing would ever get fixed in this world, because lazy people like you would just go blithely by and let things carry on unchallenged. I mean, just listen to this idiot.'

The elderly ghost reached for what appeared to be a long, thin object that had been placed on his armrest. He aimed it at the screen and started to stab it with his thumb. The volume went up further and it was like there was a tiny world inside a box with a screen, a world which was controlled by this old man. Fabian could not stretch his mind to this turn of events.

'Listen to him. What a moron! Idiot apologist!!! He has no idea! So out of touch! And that's what's wrong with this country today—no intelligence, no back bone!'

The old man pounded his walking stick on the floor.

'Now, now, Mr. Vallor.' The woman, who was obviously the man's carer, began to wag her finger at her client. 'I won't hear any more of it!'

'Just look at this monstrosity!' He coughed, thrusting the remote control at the television. '700 channels and nothing but talent shows and reality television!'

He pressed the button again. There was a tabloid

talk show hosting some random couple, making light of some ridiculous and tawdry squabble. Like most they were trying to air their dirty washing before an audience of jeering ghouls.

Their continued arguments were listened to by some well known presenter who was obviously acting as both chat show host and referee to the many unsavoury types.

'What are they talking about? Really, does anybody care?' The old man began to rant as he watched the jamboree unfold on the screen. 'It's all text speak! They have such awful diction. And the language he uses! I mean, seriously! He's an imbecile! And people enjoy watching this inane twaddle, really? It's monstrous! Monstrous I tell you!'

The carer placed a cup of water in front of the elderly man, opening the palm of her hand to reveal two tiny, round, blue pills.

'Swallow!' she ordered.

'Oh, switch it off!' he shouted, stabbing at the remote's buttons.

He looked up at the carer with an expression of true indignation and proclaimed:

'The world's gone mad! Seriously, this country and its entire population is sleepwalking to its own ruin!

And I have to conform to this? Well, of course I do. It's the only sane thing to prove one's sanity by conforming. Well, fine! So be it! I'll take my medication!'

The old man snatched the glass and the two pills from the woman's hands and took his medicine.

'Nobody listens anyway! Burn the books! Burn Rabelais! Destroy Byron! Kill off Victor Hugo and that young rascal Rimbaud! Nobody wants to read the truth anymore! Not when lies are more palatable and less of a bother! We'll go merrily on our way. The blind will lead the blind. I tell you, it's not money this country needs right now. Its common sense! It's a dose of indignation. A bloody backbone!!!'

Fabian looked at Tør and then glanced back at the old man and his ward. He asked if the two ghosts were actually aware of their presence. Tør answered that it wasn't possible at all, and reminded his host that the two other people were merely holographic recordings, ghosts, and not actually real.

'Holograms?' asked the prince, only grasping a microscopic amount of the information which Tør was imparting.

'Holograms.' The ambassador confirmed with an acknowledging smile.

'He's a bit of a crabby old devil, isn't he?' Fabian said.

Tør smiled, recognising the humour in Fabian's innocence and timing.

'That was his dementia.' He explained. 'He wasn't always this abusive, or narrow minded. I remember my father telling me that his father was happy and very sincere. That he was loved and adored by most everyone. My Grandfather was a brilliant visual artist. His paintings were probably the most unique I have ever seen. Though that was before his illness set in. Of course, he always suffered a series of mental illnesses throughout his life, struggling with thoughts, with living, as well as his failing physical health. He ended up with arthritis in his hands, which I believe more than anything brought on his dysphoria.'

The holographic carer busied herself, folding linen and placing it into the basket provided.

'Once, his faith would have derived solely from art and creativity. When he lost his abilities to enjoy these things he simply turned into the man you see now. Having grappled with mental illness all through his later life he simply didn't have the capacity to cope. I think he was unhappy because he felt invisible, and for most of his life sensed that he wasn't allowed the chance to contribute in a way that was beneficial to him. He died a confused and divested old man.'

How sad, Fabian thought to himself.

Tør carried on speaking: 'Was he right in his opinions? Could one accuse him of being egotistical? Perhaps, but he helped my father see not only the waste and profligacy of our modern times and, more importantly, he made him discover that beauty was something that mankind had overlooked.'

The old hologram sat in his chair and pounded his hand continuously upon his armrest.

'Nurse! Nurse!' He raised his voice.

'I'm not a nurse.' She corrected him. 'I'm your carer. I keep telling you. Now, what do you want?'

Tør went on:

'The individual nature and purpose of man is to live, and to live one must be cheerfully aware of the present. To right the current wrongs in our world seemed pointless to my father, a waste of effort. He realised this upon the day of my grandfather's death.

'That is not to say he did not try to awaken his generation with ideas. To change the present world, to try and improve on it, my father realised was a pointless gesture. What my father tried to do and what he believed in wholeheartedly was the simple act of kindness. Nothing more. Kindness towards his fellow man by reawakening in them motivation to see the world for what it truly was, not what it had become. I said earlier that he became part of a movement, a secret society that believed in opening the floodgates of human capacity. My father realised that our full potential, our imaginations, were probably the most underdeveloped. Backed with some capital, my father started a non-profit organisation which he called the Mythkey Initiative, to create a haven for those with great vision and abilities, offering them a home, a sanctuary, if you will, where they received the freedom and funds to create and be inspired. It was his legacy to so many. My family were rich beyond measure, and he used his vast fortune to help others finally unlock their buried potential, knowing full well that society did not give a shit enough to unlock it.'

The old man mumbled something under his breath and finally the TV was turned off.

'So what did your father gain from this act of altruism?' Fabian asked.

'Nothing. Nothing other than peace of mind. Man's greatest purpose on earth is to offer kindness to others. He gave the artists a sanctuary, as well as free time and purpose, and in the end they rewarded him with works: fine works that even to this day remain in his vast collection.'

Finally, the old man, this hologram that had

remained unaware in his modest little coffin, sat back in his chair. His hard features were beginning to soften, though his eyes told a poignant story. He glanced over to the window, the same window that every now and then revealed a tiny smile and a vigorous little wave. He missed not seeing that smile. He longed for his dear grandchild. Yearned to hear the tiny voice and feel the love that always commenced with a hug.

'When is my grandson coming to visit?' he asked the woman, the carer who was at that moment sorting through a container that supplied a cocktail of pills. She then started organising the individual pills into a clear plastic box. Each compartment was marked by a day of the week which was a reminder that the patient had taken his medicine that day.

She shrugged.

'When was it he came last?' he asked.

'How should I know?' she answered, oblivious to the old man's sudden state of mind. 'I don't live here.'

The old man was silent. Maybe it was too insignificant to tell, but Tør was certain he could see a tear trickle down the old man's face.

'There's an old human saying,' the ambassador said somberly, 'never put off today what you can do tomorrow.'

Fabian was taking in every word, every expression, and every emotion. He began to fathom in his own mind at least what was going on here. It was obvious really. The old man was lonely. He was getting on and the fact that he was surrounded by strangers, the professional type that retained no family ties and no emotional ties did not help matters either.

Tør shook his head regretfully.

'We, that is, my father and I, maybe only visited 3, perhaps 4 or 5 times a year, and then only during holidays. Business always kept my father from visiting more often.'

'I suppose you lament that…now.' Fabian offered.

'I regret a lot of things, most of which were situations out of my control. But, you know, if I had been a little older I might have come here on my own. It would have made this old goat's day.'

Fabian folded his arms as he stepped nearer to Tør.

'I don't wish to sound insensitive, my friend,' the prince said, resting his hand gently on Tør's shoulder, 'but he's a facsimile, the past, you have told me this yourself. You and I, we are the now. We're alive. We are real and we are part of the present. If anything, we should try to leave old regrets where they belong: in the past. Don't you think?'

The emissary smiled broadly. Maybe this medieval boy, this young man of limited learning was beginning to understand.

'You're right…You are so right. I cry for ghosts. I lament for holograms that are no longer the living. It is true. And I talk about things that are really not important anymore.

Fabian noticed the timer on the top of the cube as it started to turn counter clockwise, and quickly remembered to close his eyes.

When he opened them again he quickly realised he was outside. Only this time it was day. And the world still appeared strange and alien to him. He was sitting on some sort of chair at some form of table. The frame was made of metal and the flat surface was composed of a polished glass. In the distant backdrop rose a Gothic cathedral which stood in contrast to the structures surrounding it.

'Where have you brought us now?' Fabian queried.

'This, my friend, is the city of Paris.'

The happy laughter of some children playing mingled with the sound of people talking, recounting the day they had enjoyed with friends or loved ones. Fabian saw an old man reading a newspaper at another table, and then began to observe a couple kissing. But it was the two young men who walked by, hand in hand, and very much in love that turned Fabian's head. That was probably the first shock, the first revelation, an epiphany that hit him more than this alien environment, more than the technology or magic that Tør had conjured from his so-called holographic cube.

Open mouthed, Fabian looked at the ambassador with a huge question written all over his face.

'I see that that image has moved you.' The ambassador noticed. 'I see that this has been a secret longing you have grappled with, for how long I cannot say. It is understandable that you would be pleasantly shocked considering the sheltered life you have led.'

Fabian watched as the two lovers sat down and ordered drinks from a table waiter. As the attendant walked casually away with their orders, the two other men began to drink in the sights. This city was full of amazing locations, filled with fervour and infatuation. Fabian watched intensely as the two male lovers held hands, looking deep into each other's eyes, and drew nearer, moreover they began to kiss. Strange that no one else seemed to batt an eyelid. Fabian was captivated by their apparent brazenness.

'No one thinks this is strange, two men walking openly hand in hand? No one is giving it a second thought!'

'And why should they?' Tør asked.

'I don't know—because it isn't normal?'

'I'd spare you the cliché of having to ask you the question: what is normal? Normal is whatever feelings you have. There is nothing more natural than love. These two men love each other. Only a fool would question otherwise.'

Fabian was silent as he glanced at the two men.

Tør was sombre as he read the changing expressions on his host's face. Finally, he could see. He began to speak thus:

'It must have been so restricting for you: knowing you had these feelings, but not knowing how to express them, or not knowing if you should dare. You must have believed these feelings were nothing more than an irregular fancy. Especially when no one around you seemed to harbour the same feelings. But it's true, there are indeed places, people, things that you could not even imagine, and, yes, anything is possible. Close your eyes.'

As he heard these words, Fabian did what he was told. He could now feel the ambassador's breath on his skin and saw the brief flash through his eyelids. Present sounds seemed to disappear and were quickly replaced by a strange rhythm, a loud beat, performed by a number of musical instruments he could not identify. Even the aroma in the air had changed dramatically. He coughed. The air was thick with smoke and dry. When Fabian finally opened his eyes he was standing in a room full of people. The only lights that were available seemed to rock and gyrate from secret compartments in the ceiling above them.

People's bodies were moving to the music, and even more disconcerting was the fact that Tør had his arms looped over Fabian's shoulders in the most romantic pose. He felt a sudden rush of conflicting emotions.

'Don't be frightened.' Tør told him. 'Let me be your guide. Look at my eyes.'

The moment Fabian looked directly at those beautiful eyes he immediately tensed.

'Loosen up. Come on. Look, if you are half as curious about life as I know you are you're going to have to loosen up a bit. Watch me. Watch my feet.'

'If...if this is just an illusion' Fabian stammered. 'Then we are still in my father's arboretum. What if someone sees us like this? What if my father sees us?'

'No one is going to see us. Don't worry. No one will come into the arboretum, and no one is going to find us. Everyone is at the celebration.'

Overwhelmed with conflicting feelings, Fabian decided to do as he was told. He stared down at Tør's feet and followed his steps.

'You see. Now you're getting it! Now look at me.'

That final requisite turned out to be fatal. At that very second, as their eyes locked on each other, Fabian felt stirrings that suddenly begged those barriers to fall. Their lips met in a passionate kiss. The sudden adrenaline rush caused the most unexpected thing to happen. It was terrifying only to Fabian because he had noticed it. Tør had his eyes shut and therefore was unaware. But Fabian's eyes began to turn blood red. He felt it, almost similar to the sensation he had discovered earlier that day in the woods when he came upon the child and the carnivorous plant.

Yes, the dragon within was feeling the Adrenaline too. He had to hold the monster back somehow. He closed his eyes tighter than before and Tør suddenly felt the tension in Fabian's muscles. Their lips parted and Tør could see that Fabian was struggling, though against what he could not say.

With a voice barely audible, Fabian said:

'Y-You never told me what happened to your world.'

This was random. But what seemed arbitrary in this case was only a disguised, if a slightly agitated attempt to hold the demons back, to stop the dragon from surfacing.

Panic ensued, though Fabian did his best to conceal it.

'Does it matter?' the ambassador said, looking at him oddly. 'I just didn't wish to spoil this moment.'

His skin perspiring, Fabian merely regarded the ambassador with a look that demanded an answer. Tør confessed that he was confused by the response of his host.

'Tell me what happened,' the prince insisted as he backed away.

Confused by this unwarranted outburst, Tør finally realised that this whole experience must have been overwhelming to say the least.

'My world died,' he said, finally. 'It died because even in a world of promised beauty and an abundance of liberty there are monsters. Monsters consume fire until their very nature consumes all within their path.'

Suddenly the holographic world around them began to melt away. It took a small while for Fabian to remember that it was just an illusion anyway and that they were still in the arboretum under the stars.

The two stood there for a minute before Fabian could sum up the courage to tell him:

'Thank you.'

'For what?'

'For showing me that world. For showing me that there is much more to life than the confines of this place. Do you know what? My father never once let me travel out beyond those woods. If I tried he'd always send his guards in after me to drag me back in disgrace. Life here isn't exactly perfect.' Fabian added.

The prince thought hard about what he was going to say next.

'I don't feel as though I fit in here. I feel alone here. My father is always abusive towards me. He has been ever since my mother died. He hates me. I know he does.'

It was at this point where Fabian felt he had said too much and should shut his mouth. He looked down at the ground, finding it difficult at that moment to make eye contact with Tør. There was fresh evidence in his eyes that suggested he was close to losing his composure. Despite his misgivings however he continued:

'I...I feel like I don't belong anymore. I feel like I am a bird that has somehow outgrown the cage but is not permitted to leave. I'm sorry. I'm not making much sense. I admit I'm not as eloquent with words as you are. And I have witnessed these marvels. I can see and touch but cannot hold onto them. The joy you have shown me. I cannot keep it. I cannot have it.'

Tør showed no sign at all that he was going to snub the prince for his honesty, or his inhibitions.

'The world I came from,' he said finally, 'was not shy of these desires and needs, not by any means.'

The Ambassador drew nearer to his host, making the prince feel a sudden rush of uneasiness once again.

'I have seen the way you looked at me.' He observed, lifting his hand gently to touch a whorl of the prince's hair, lightly brushing it to one side. Fabian might have felt a sudden pang of shame were it not for the warmth he felt rising up from his loins. It was irresistible and felt forbidden, and for one overpowering moment he discovered that he was no longer just a solitary soul bitterly denigrated to loneliness. He was in love. It was a totally new experience, one which defined him in a different way than he had known.

'Eloquence isn't needed,' Tør said tenderly. 'I recognised that you were not entirely happy the moment I saw you in the great hall. Sometimes our eyes betray a story our mouths dare not impart. You don't have to explain.'

Fabian felt his heart swell as they kissed.

* * *

The king, who had decided to take his momentary leave to enjoy the gardens surrounding his castle, spied the two fraternising forms standing at a distance in the moonlight. René could barely believe his eyes. His son was in the arms of the ambassador! He did not act, could not act, for fear of raising the ambassador's disapproval, and, consequently, harming any relations with the mighty and terrible Sinistrom. He backed stealthily away, choosing not to believe the evidence before his eyes.

Chapter 4

The banquet was finally over. Talks were to begin at day break. It was agreed. In the meantime, some of the Sinistrom forces returned to camp, while others disbanded, making the long journey back to base.

Night's obsidian veil had already descended upon the southern hemisphere in which the dark citadel stood. Its stark black towers reached outwards toward the vile smelling ether, clogged by the curtain of methane and mist.

This was home to the loathsome Viper Masters and their cruel leader, Malecarjan.

The red eyed John Dafoe, emissary and adviser to King Kardas Vallor, made his presence felt to the reptilian warriors present. Unable to breathe the atmosphere, he appeared before them as a projection.

'I need to speak to Malecarjan. Where is he?' the hologram inquired.

Tai Pan, a large snake-like warrior, garbed in a type of armour that looked curiously similar to a samurai's

Lamellar plating, rolled his tongue over his left eye, then snapped his lids shut, wiping away any saliva that might have been left there. The vile henchman spoke thus:

'My massssster is in recessss and will not be available until the rissssing of the ssssun, your Lordship'.

The enigma was not altogether satisfied with this answer, though he guessed it was to be expected.

Ophidia, Malecarjan's callous warrior maiden, interjected before the displeased enigma could speak.

'He is in recessss and does not wish to be disssturbed. However, if it is urgent I will be more than prepared to passss the message on to his Lordssship.'

Her show of daring was lost on the holographic man who stood before her. The enigma was master and his authority was not about to be challenged by any snake. Suddenly, his eyes appeared to roll up into his head, leaving only the whites visible. It was as if he was entering a possessed state of reverie or trance. The other serpents began to back away with fear as they had seen the enigma do this before, and fully knew the consequences. As they watched, a descending crease emerged along the hologram's forehead. Flesh parted, separating along the sustained fold. Then a hollow fissure appeared above the man's eye line. A clear mucous dripped lazily from the punctured skin that folded back along his brow like sepals. Out of it grew a parasitic being. Long, red, with a network of sinews and veins, the strange being stretched outwards beyond the host's forehead, and stopped. A single bud at the tip of the crimson stalk flowered into the shape of an eye, peering round; discerning the entourage of snakes stood cowering before it.

This third eye, this protrusion, began to speak directly into the minds of its servants.

'I shall return for your leader, Malecarjan. I am power personified, and I will not tolerate disobedience! Understood? We are on the cusp of a great victory and though this fact pleases me greatly, I find myself at odds with your lack of reverence. See to it this does not happen again.'

The servants clutched at their heads in a useless bid to ward off the discomfort forced upon them by this parasite.

The holographic image of John Dafoe spun round. As it did so it vanished like a ghost. Ophidia blinked and continued to stare at the spot where the John and the parasitic eye had stood.

Malecarjan knew that his lord was unhappy with him. He too was unhappy and disdainful of his master's rather egalitarian tactics. After all, what use was an army that had been bred for war if all they did was sit idly by as their masters signed treaties of peace? What good was a weapon if all it did was sit gathering dust? Malecarjan was just such a weapon, and he did not like the thought of being someone's play thing. Though, instead of opposing the orders appointed by his betters, he resolved to meet with his sorcerer and adviser, the ancient witch known to many as Lady Creepsake.

The witch dwelled deep in the caverns beneath the dark tower. Malecarjan needed a plan of action and he hoped the witch could give him one.

In her customary manner Lady Creepsake appeared in her monster form, casting a shadow of her outline against the cavern wall. She herself could not be seen amidst the clutter: the mountains of gems, and statues, and flaming braziers that gave off a dim, orange flicker. The strange shape in the dim glow appeared long, bulbous, an undulating silhouette with many insect-like appendages. This was Lady Creepsake's true form. The giant centipede with her hundred gangly legs began to rear up on its haunches. Malecarjan could not see her physical shape, though could discern that she was putting on her robes from the shadow she cast, looming larger as she approached. At last,

Malecarjan got the first glimpse of her. She was no longer a centipede. She was for the moment bipedal, or at least offering the appearance she was thus. She had six arms, a female torso and pelvis; a far cry from the multi segmented form of her counter appearance. This suggested that the hundred or so legs were either hidden by her robes or were otherwise concealed by magic.

'Speak not, my Lord,' she told him respectfully. 'I look within your soul and already I can see your determination. Thou harboureth designs against our present master, though fear his wrath.'

The woman wore a veil which hid the mandibles beneath with startling ease. Only her seductive eyes peered through, glinting like two finely polished, emerald pearls.

'I see now what you must do.'

Malecarjan's appearance, much like hers, was concealed by both veil and magic.

'Tell me, my lady. I need guidance,' he said.

'No, all you need is stealth—Stealth and cunning.'

With a single gesture of her hand she cast a wicked spell of vision against the cavern wall. Betwixt the light that surrounded the vision a picture of Prince Fabian appeared. It was a depiction of mortal terror, framed by the many grasping vines which had entangled themselves round his arms and legs. Malecarjan watched as the vision unfolded.

'This,' said the witch, 'is a glimpse of the recent past. Now watch.'

The carnivorous plant in the vision was close to devouring the two would-be victims, only something truly astonishing happened. The prince began to go through a remarkable and shocking metamorphosis. In a matter of moments human flesh and pigmentation had given way to a fiery red, and a tough shield of scales had at once replaced soft skin.

'He's a dragon!'

The Lord, Malecarjan could barely believe his eyes.

'Now watch!'

The witch cast another image against the stone. This time it showed the two young men, the prince and the ambassador, fraternizing in the gardens surrounding the palace.

'Tør!' said Malecarjan with distaste. 'He treats our enemy like a lover. It's sickening!'

Lady Creepsake discontinued the vision with a quick flick of her hand.

'The prince of Mundor, Fabian is his name,' she rasped. 'He clandestinely harbours a monstrous secret, and thus becomes a monster and steals his lover away. Think of it. It is the perfect opportunity. Our Lord, Kardas, rallies his armies and, in a fit of rage, lays siege to the kingdom of Mundor in a desperate bid to avenge his son's capture. Malecarjan, what you have here is the perfect occasion to make Prince Fabian the scapegoat, the centre of attention. With a little magic you could make all Mundor believe that he kidnapped Tør. It is perfect! It is delicious.'

The witch laughed in rasps and shrieks.

'It cannot fail!'

Already there was a plan formulating in Malecarjan's head. Yes, he thought, discredit Fabian. Make him look like the villain. Make him and his father appear degenerate in the eyes of Kardas Vallor. War would then be inevitable.

Tweak sat on the floor, staring at the magic mirror. He had seen the vision too. For a whole day he sat there, staring at the looking glass as though in a trance. The full shock of it had not fully hit home, though he seemed unable to pull himself round. The prince was a monster! The heir to the throne of Mundor was a dragon! So that was why he had been hauled back, man handled by the king's men, stark-naked, with nothing more than a scant cloth to hide his shame, and that was why he was silent and acting so strangely.

Shaking off his daze, Tweak wondered what he would do. Would he rat on the prince and tell King René the news? No. Not only would that be folly, it would be dishonourable as well. True, the king would not believe him. And René had enough worries without this recent situation becoming public knowledge.

Tweak sat for a good long while pondering the question.

Finally, rising to his feet, he decided to go and confront the prince himself. There had to be some kind of rational explanation for this transformation, something that would put his mind at rest. Even though this hideous alchemy was evil, Tweak knew Fabian to be a good, honest man.

Malecarjan returned to his soldiers with a new plan. Ophidia was eager to watch her master return from Lady Creepsake's parlour, though was not happy to impart the news. She explained that the enigma, special envoy to Kardas, had visited in spirit – and wished to speak to him immediately.

Malecarjan growled with frustration. *I have no time to waste on that Sinistrom fool*, he thought to himself.

'He has powersss.' Ophidia cautioned him. 'He isss a man not to be trifled with. Do not forget hisss people created usss.'

'And yet our so-called masters make peace! You are correct in what you say. Yes. It was John Dafoe's race – the tribe known as the Orcons – who made us. Took DNA from reptiles and merged it with the human genome. Created and engineered us. Never forget that, Ophidia, my vicious beauty. And never forget that it was our high lord, Kardas – he whom the Orcons serve – who tried to stop Dafoe from conducting his illegal experiment.'

'I have never forgotten,' Ophidia said.

'Good, because Kardas is a hypocrite,' he said. 'Just as all of his people are hypocrites. Politics is the air they breathe. Morality, the very lie they tell themselves.'

Ophidia lowered her eyes. She knew deep down that what Malecarjan said was the truth.

Malecarjan continued his hateful diatribe:

'Kardas finally took it upon himself to pardon Dafoe. So basically John was spared the penalty for his crimes and we were spared our fates as well. We were allowed to live out our existence as abominations. Rather than destroy us – a fate that would have been much kinder – Kardas decided to exploit our ferocity. Our Power!'

Ophidia also knew this was true. She remained silent, however.

Malecarjan pivoted on the balls of his feet. His long cloak rose and swung behind him in a dramatic flurry of crimson.

'That is their weakness.' He deduced. 'The unyielding belief that they alone hold power. These irresistible humans! They are the confirmed, undeniable bloodlines. They have run like a river of sewage through the veins of this world. They make me shudder, these royal beings. They are truly weak. We are the real power here. We only have to believe that we are and believe in ourselves.'

'We are weapons.' Ophidia looked away thoughtfully. 'Fashioned and honed. Nothing more than living deterrents.'

'This makes me furious! This makes me rage!' Malecarjan snarled. 'What use is a weapon that is never used? We are not warriors. We are simply a means to achieving peace. We sit here at the behest of our masters while they talk of armistice. And we simply rot in the darkness while they sit in opulence and live like kings in the beautiful niches of the world.'

Malecarjan made a gesture to Tai Pan, his shape shifting right hand. Tai Pan approached steadily, knowing that his lord was not in the best of moods.

'I want you to put on a disguise,' Malecarjan instructed. 'I want you to go to Mundor, and I want you to cause a diversion. This is the shape, the very form I want you to assume. Now look.'

Malecarjan opened the palm of his hand. Out sprang a magical vision, tiny though quite detailed. It flickered and gambolled much like a flame. It was a vision of a dragon, though no ordinary dragon. This was the one noted as the Dragon Tolan. It hovered momentarily above Malecarjan's hand, a hallucination or mental image. Tai Pan saw the facsimile of the fearsome Tolan and considered this a task worthy of his abilities. As a shape shifter, and a trickster, Tai Pan had the facility to make himself great or small and could make himself look like anyone, irrespective of age or species.

'At once, my lord,' he said, bowing his head.

It was market day in Mundor. The streets were heaving with the usual entourage of buyers and merchants. Prince Fabian caught the sudden scent of strong herbs as he and Tør ambled slowly through the crowds. He and the young emissary had only just met, but they were getting to know each other in a way that would allow their love to blossom.

Neither of them saw the furtive eyes watching them from behind a selection of dream catchers. A moustached stranger, wearing a hood and a cloak, seemed to display an invested interest in the regally dressed pair.

'So' began Fabian, picking up a couple of apples from a vender's table and handing some silver coins to the merchant. 'How long are you going to be staying with us at the castle?'

He handed the ambassador the other apple as they continued to walk.

'Until the talks are complete and our two respective peoples can finally see eye to eye.'

'I don't get it.' Fabian looked understandably confused. 'Aside from your associates, you don't strike me as the sort of person that would subscribe to fear and conquest, much less condone it. Yet you have conquered these people. Clearly you have used similar tactics in order to add these other races to your military might.'

Tør allowed a smile to play across his face.

'If we had simply come to you, a handful of men, unarmed, unassuming—would your king have really listened to a request for alliance? I doubt it. At least under a flag of truce we can begin to recognise a common objective. We can share peace. We can offer an education, far more superior than you have known. We can improve your lives.'

Fabian thought for a second.

'You talk of peace. But I think you are confusing peace with ruling. You want to control us. You want to influence us. Why? Because you believe we are backwards? You think, just because we live in castles, and use simple implements to farm with, and you have objects that can conjure ghosts out of thin air, that we somehow need improvement. Forced improvement?'

Tør was a little longer in responding to this challenge.

'Believe what you will,' he said. 'Whatever you might think of me— whatever you may think of my race; and you must not spread what I say to anyone else. This goes no further. I trust you, Fabian. The truth is your people were never meant to live in castles, or huts, behind walls of cold stone. You were never supposed to be firing muskets or using large broadswords in battle. You, like us, once lived in tower blocks, magnificently tall buildings made of glass. You had chariots made of metal, with combustion systems, and technology to get you from one corner of the world to the other in less time it would take you now. Your people were like us once. You had weapons too. Hydrogen bombs. Nuclear bombs. Now, these things you've never even heard of.

Why? Because at one point in your history you lost it all. You were driven back to the dark ages. All that scientific knowledge just disappeared. It is something that nearly happened on our world too. On Earth wars were fought. A lot of people died. Most of our great minds were lost. A handful of us lived on and fled to the stars in the hopes of making a new home for ourselves. And we landed here. All those years ago. I suppose we feel responsible for you. And that is why we intervene. It is because we care. Now that the peace talks will soon be underway, my presence will be needed in a short while after my recess. And then the real work can begin with the full cooperation of your people.'

'And then you'll be leaving us, I suppose?'

The young emissary caught the look of disappointment on his host's face.

'Yes. I have to…But we can still be friends.'

The young prince was still not happy with the news. Secretly he wished they could be more than just passing acquaintances.

'You know,' began Fabian, continuing their earlier conversation, 'I've been thinking about what you were saying regarding our past.'

'Yes?' Tør raised an eyebrow.

'We know about the remnants. On occasion I have

seen bits and pieces strewn along the ground, in the woods, in fields. There are places that we are not meant to enter as we have been told they contain dangers, ghosts from a forgotten time which we would not understand. I have seen metal debris and have speculated about its purpose. So what were you saying about this thing that happened to my people, this change that occurred? Are you saying that all that debris—we left it? That it is there because of us?'

Tør gave his host a knowing smile.

'That "debris" as you call it, it was left by your people, yes. Many years ago, your world was shaken by an unnatural disaster. As such, as the number of people able to understand science became fewer, you began to retire to more simplistic modes of survival. Here in the wilderness your forebears took to using quill instead of pen, and the sword instead of weapons of mass destruction. When that happened a lot of the old technology was left, as you described, strewn along the ground like litter. But just take a look around you, your people were never meant to live this way. This is not the plan. This is not the natural part of your development. Take a look at this marketplace for example. Over there—' and he pointed to a stall where a woman was selling wooden utensils.

'A few centuries ago that woman's great, great, great grandmother might have been selling appliances, machines capable of blending and crushing fruit to a liquid. The only things here which she sells are mortars and pestles and wooden spoons. And over at that stall there, you see a goldsmith. He's selling jewellry. Notice how bulky those trinkets are? And look there, over by the fountain. The stall with the dresses and the shirts and trousers. All of these things look crudely manufactured, and basic. Why? If you could see the times of development in which you people lived, you would see wonders, as well as much finer things. Now all you're left with are remnants, things you no longer understand. Things you fear.'

'My father rarely talks about the oddities we've seen littered around our kingdom. He doesn't even like me talking about it.'

'There you go you see,' Tør replied. 'Fear of what is not known. You cannot let fear stop you. And you cannot let anyone tell you that you are wrong. Not even your father. If you do they will always hold power over you. Do you understand?'

'Yes.' Fabian hesitated.

The two young men continued to walk through the bustling market place, unaware of the mustached stranger. This stranger remained still as though waiting, expecting something to happen. His eyes were wide and sustained a constant, uneasy vigil on the street up ahead. He was not alone in his covert endeavor. He was waiting for a sign. A distraction. He knew something was about to happen.

In the midst of the flurry of people and the countless voices that encompassed the market streets a single loud cry was heard. Unexpectedly, people began to scatter, giving rise to the very object of their terror: a horse had been pulling a cart when suddenly it was spooked. The load bearing animal was on a wild rampage through the cobbled streets. Its hooves thundered as they hammered the ground, charging in the direction of a small child.

'Look out!' someone shouted.

The little boy only responded by turning his head in the direction of the commotion.

Prince Fabian thought very little of his own safety, and ran out into the path of the horse, grasping the child. The prince leaped clean out of the way just as the animal barrelled past. The child was safe.

Another spy emerged from behind one of the stalls. Lady Creepsake, disguised as an elderly woman, made a swift gesture with her hand. A silent spell was cast.

Fabian was about to pick himself up. Many people began to flock round the child, asking if he was alright, as well as enquiring if he was scared. They seemed to pay no attention to the prince who had risked his life to save him. And no one witnessed the prince as he vanished seemingly into thin air. There was no trace of him. The darkest magic had spirited him away.

Time for the next phase of the operation, the old lady thought, having done her part. She simply walked away without anyone noticing.

The hooded man with the moustache regarded his handiwork and backed away, knowing how well these little diversions sufficed in drawing people's attentions. He stood in the side-lines for a second and grinned wickedly. All was going to plan.

Shape-shifting his appearance, he took on the form of his true persona as the Viper Master trickster, Tai Pan. And then, in a further change, he began to mimic the appearance of Fabian's alter ego. The Dragon Tolan.

Tai Pan, masquerading as the great red dragon, beat his huge webbed wings, raising himself high over the pandemonium. He set the market stalls ablaze with fire, fire that filled the market square, permeating the streets with a conflagration and further panic. People fled.

Adding a little more theatricality to his power play,

Tai Pan uttered the words, mimicking Prince Fabian's voice:

'My father was always such a soft touch! But I have harnessed the dragon's heart. Have tasted it and will not bow to invaders...'

Tai Pan soared high and banked for another pass. This time he had the ambassador in his sights.

'...not even one as deceptively beautiful as you!' he roared, swooping towards the ground, and lifting the screaming youth in his talons. The royal guards, who had only just arrived at the scene, fired their arrows at the sky, but the dragon was far too fast for them and was gone, leaving the bowmen out of range.

Tweak, who had also been at the market that morning, had witnessed the rescue. He was then frustrated by the sudden movement of the crowds, obscuring his vision.

'Fabian?'

That call, delivered from Tweak's lips like the very progeny of betrayal and defilement, hung in the air as the dust settled. A bell sounded as the town's people began to douse the flames with water, collected from the local well.

Chapter 5

The white temple of Sun Haven stood in a hollow between two hills. Some say it was the most beautiful place in all the hemispheres, though few had ever set foot in this corner of paradise and even fewer had ever left to tell about it. Not because it was full of danger, but because the traveller never wanted to leave. This place was literally a haven of peace, a place wherein its leaders, blessed with a timeless wisdom, ruled all the other kingdoms with charity, prudence, and, above all, respect.

This was the place where law and government began. Behind a shroud of mystery this one kingdom remained the one true bastion of progress and technology. It was a kingdom hidden from the rest of the world by a mighty barrier of energy. Only those who were advanced enough to understand these wonders could gain entry. Within its powerful walls lay many secrets that were rarely shared, even with those considered allies. For that was the basis of their wisdom. It was a haven created by one Kardas Vallor, the one true king who reigned over twelve realms of this world. This temple was his home.

It was a six day journey from King René's territory on horseback, yet news travelled fast. A red robin flitted from the window, finally perching itself next to an old man seated by an inglenook and a roaring fire. The elderly man, known to his peers as Kardas, who these days sat, stroking a mane of white facial hair and talking gently to forest animals, allowed the tiny bird to come near. Craning his neck somewhat, the old man listened to what the robin had to tell him.

'No,' Kardas said, his voice broken, though audible to the tiny robin, the messenger who could see the scowl deepening on his lord's face.

'No! My son was taken by a dragon? Where is he now?'

The robin did not speak. Instead the answer came from another voice, another presence of which the great Kardas was previously unaware.

'In the Marshes of Mundor, my king,' announced the new voice.

The old man turned slowly toward the creature that had just spoken.

'And who might you be?'

The creature, a small rabbit, bounded in through the door of the temple and said:

'Who I am is not important. The news I bring you, my Lord Kardas, is. Your son was taken by none other than Prince Fabian. He has the ability to transform himself into a great dragon. He has left a blaze, a trail along the land.'

'That would be a lie, my little friend.' The elderly gentleman was clearly in denial. 'Firstly, I doubt the prince of Mundor has such a fanciful ability. Second, King René and I are presently in peace talks. Any act of violence on their part would be stupid. It would lead to war, a prospect neither I nor King René would-'

'My king,' interrupted the rabbit, 'Prince Fabian is in love with your son and is also fearful of his father's prejudices. I fear he has acted irrationally. He has acted alone.'

The king raised an eyebrow.

'He has left a fiery trail, you say?'

The robin lent forward while perched on the old man's shoulder and chirped the facts into his ear.

Kardas listened intently to the robin. His eyes, wise beyond mortal years, widened with surprise. But the robin had never lied before. So finally Kardas conceded. This was a world rich in magic after all.

'Fly,' commanded the old man finally, looking at the robin on his shoulder. 'Fly to my agents in the southern hemisphere. Fly with all haste to the dark citadel and tell my armies to prepare, but do nothing, not until I have tried to resolve this issue with King René himself. Go!'

The tiny robin took to the air, flying straight to the open window. The rabbit too had gone, vanished before the old man had even noticed his absence.

Outside in the forest, in a small clearing, the bird and the rabbit both metamorphosed back into their original forms.

Tai Pan turned to Creepsake, the witch, and glared at all the raw beauty around them.

'This is what we were bred to defend, this paradise. Yet those who command our loyalty let us live in darkness and squalor while the great and wise old man lives like a god amidst such splendour!'

'Correct,' said Madam Creepsake, hatching a devious plot. 'That is why Lord Malecarjan sent us two here as his messengers. When finally the realm of Mundor begins to distrust us, and when news of Fabian's villainy reaches the 12 realms, then warriors of the 12 kingdoms will force King René to abdicate. By which time Kardas, the great and wise, will try to intervene.

He doesn't want a war. But try as he might, his voice will wither, and his authority will wane. The people of a dozen realms will want to avenge Tør's abduction, even though his father will not. I know people. I know how they react. They will drop their leaders with ease if they feel strongly enough about it. Then you and your snakes will move in and take what is rightfully yours.'

'You are cunning,' said Tai Pan.

'Indeed,' replied the witch. 'Now go. Return to the kingdom of Mundor. Transform back to your dragon form. Make sure you are seen. See that the people witness your transformation back into the prince and then there can be no question.'

'At once, my lady.'

The snake stepped back a few paces, transforming himself into the dragon form once again.

In no time at all, the trickster's great dragon wings carried him high above the trees, above the encampments that flanked the kingdom. He alighted at long last, landing squarely atop the battlements and made certain people saw his swift conversion into a likeness of the prince. He strutted along the parapets, a cunning smile upon his lips. He physically vanished into air, leaving the few observers with no clue as to his departure.

The pristine and ostentatious council chamber came to life as the two main doors slid open to admit the humble Kardas. The doors, much like the walls to this entire room resembled frosted glass, pure and white, and vaguely transparent. Strange writing adorned the partitions and glowed white with an almost heavenly zeal. In fact, this whole room seemed rather divine and alive with a wonderful and unearthly glow.

The lord and ruler of this realm stepped into the chamber. Several hollow tubes flanked him on either side, like tall columns that seemed to reach upwards towards the sky since the great hall had no ceiling. They appeared to be made of a material like glass, though they were actually made of a much different material, alien in nature.

Inside each tube a ghostly image appeared. A man dressed in robes, and then another figure, this time a woman clothed in similar manner, materialized like out of thin air, inside one column, then another, and another, and another, until all the symmetrical columns were occupied by a holographic representation of each councillor.

"Speak, my lord," requested one of the holographic councillors.

Kardas regarded each of the faces as they regarded him. They looked wise, wise beyond their years which were in truth indeterminate. Looking at the one whom he recognised and regarded as a close friend, he said:

'He has taken my son, this Mundorian Prince. He has kidnapped my son and is holding him I know not where.'

The holographic face of his friend, the councillor known as Jacob, closed his eyes tightly and shook his head disagreeably.

After a short pause he looked back down at the tiny speck of a man before him and said, 'This had to be. You know full well my opinion on the subject, but you had to push it to its limit, did you not?'

'Jacob, I-'

But before Kardas could utter another word the holographic figure in the tall cylinder column said:

'No, Kardas. I said what would happen, and this council chose to ignore my warnings. This society which you plan to mould with your bare hands is still young, still newborn. What gave us the right to meddle in their affairs?'

Kardas raised a hand.

'Who is meddling? We have ruled the other twelve realms with wisdom and benevolence. And we agreed that we would not release or share technology that would inevitably tarnish their natural development. We all agreed to a declaration, an edict forbidding us to do so. Now, my esteemed colleague here pays lip service to what he deems correct with this, his latest exposé.'

Jacob's face turned quickly into a frown.

'But our very presence here contaminates this world. The very act of influencing politics here on Mundoria is proof enough that you have turned a situation to chaos.'

Kardas looked bemused.

'I disagree.' He countered. 'Don't forget. We caused the problems on this world. Or don't you remember? It was the presence of our own ship's drive systems that triggered this world to lose its own use of technology. The singularity which we produced when we arrived in orbit caused an event that triggered the eventual fall of these people. Because of us, they lost their identity. Because of us, they now live like primitives. Do they not deserve our help? Our guidance? Well? Don't you think we have a responsibility to teach them? Patch things up at least.'

'Listen to him,' Jacob continued, now gazing ahead at all his fellow council members, 'we are no better than all the invaders throughout our dark and bloody history who have interfered with the natural growth of lesser developed cultures. And in truth they are less developed regardless of whether they were once progressive. The twelve other kingdoms which we managed to annex were nothing more than barbarians, hordes, and ruffians. Monsters even! Some of them! I don't blame King René or his son for doubting our intentions. He fears us. You have created a construct of fear.'

'No,' agued Kardas. 'It it is not fear, it is strength. Without strength one cannot affect politics.'

'It is fear. René has always feared the might of the other kingdoms. You came along and united them against him, effectively. What did you think you would achieve? Just take a look at our so-called progressive actions throughout history. The hypocrisy of your argument, dear Kardas, is nothing short of staggering. Have we not learned from our mistakes? We were once flesh. I and the other council members present here today were once bone, blood, and sinew. Now look at what we have become. Many of us chose our immortality based on nothing more than a fad, a wish fulfillment inaugurated by the rich and influential to gain more riches from a gullible mob. We who are no longer flesh now pay the ultimate price for our lack of intelligence and our vanity. We think of ourselves as ascended beings. We are now made up of light. Our form which you see has no capability of touch, or taste, or smell, no feeling at all. And here we have resided for years beyond measure. And we call ourselves wise?'

'That is enough, Jacob,' said another council member.

'You are right, Councillor Talon,' continued Jacob. 'It is enough. But time will reveal the truth. And the truth is we are not ready ourselves. How can we possibly dictate to these barbarians the right way of living, if we have no idea ourselves? All we are doing is digging a deeper hole into which we shall fall, imperceptibly, into the pit of our own making.'

Kardas kept his head raised to the towering ghost of Jacob.

'This rant is beneath you, my friend councillor,' said the old man who was more flesh and blood than any of his contemporaries. 'You speak of us as though we have done a serious wrong—a rape no less. Indeed, the only real mistake we made was creating this dilemma in the first place. We made a grievous error in our calculations and these people paid the price. It is our responsibility, nay, our duty, to respond by educating them.'

'And they have taken your son,' Jacob reminded him, cutting the old man short. 'Tell me, do you still wish to help and educate them? You already know you cannot do this by force! You undermine everything. And what are you teaching them? Simply that we are a power they are obliged to fear. But fear does not promote teaching, or wisdom. It has the opposite effect as King René has obviously proven by taking your own flesh and blood. Now what do you say to that?'

'I have shown force,' said Kardas. 'And yes, I have shown strength and sternness. Tell me, what teacher has not displayed austerity regarding a difficult lesson? But War, my friends, is the farthest thing from my mind. We must annex all the kingdoms of this world in order so that we can unite them. I will make a show of force if necessary, but I will not take a realm by force.'

'Are you really that naïve? Looks to me like you have already lost this battle. It would appear war is inevitable. Until now, René has shown that he and his people are far from being weak and inferior. You won't be able to sway their thinking by peaceful means. I am sorry, my friend, but you are on your own in this matter and I believe I speak for every other council member here. I hope very much that you can find a peaceful solution to resolve this situation. But I doubt that there is one.'

With that the council members vanished.

Kardas turned to walk away. As he made his exit from

the council chamber he was greeted by a subordinate. This aide was a technician, a young male of about twenty years. Blond curly hair framed a cherubic complexion. A pair of limpid blue eyes looked up at the old man as he gave his report:

'We have completed an analysis of the rout the dragon took.'

'And?' said Kardas, filled with excitement and expectation.

The young aid had that look of reluctance in his eyes suddenly.

'We tracked the blaze of fire along the breadth of the land. We also took the liberty of tracing the creature's pulmonary patterns to its last known coordinates. I don't know what it was, sire, but there is something in the clouds high above the badlands that blocks our sensor technology. We cannot identify it. It is like the dragon disappeared and then returned briefly on our scanners.'

Kardas looked puzzled.

'Where is the creature now?'

'Judging by its decay ratings it flew back to Mundor where its heartbeat changed radically. It is like the heart of the great beast shrank to human size.'

Kardas turned to walk away. He had a responsibility to put all of this right. He understood that he would have to approach King René himself and ask him to explain what he had done with his son. He would have to approach king René in his holographic form. It would have to be done quickly as time was fleeting, and he had no idea what danger Tør was likely to be in, if any.

News reached the court of King René.
'They are without principle!'
The king rose from his throne. After hearing about the tragedy that had taken place in his own market square, he called for his councillors to attend a meeting.
'King Kardas Vallor himself appeared in my chambers just a short while ago,' he told them. 'He presented himself as some kind of spirit! I tell you, I could see the room behind him visibly through his clothes. He was as clear in appearance as bloody gossamer! He projected himself into my room and had the devil to ask me about my son! He requested to see him. Well, I said to him that I was stunned that he wasn't more interested in what had happened to his own son. This whole business has to be the work of a demon, or witch! Really, am I to believe a dragon attacked my market square? Am I to trust the word of a few dozen people, claiming they heard this dragon speak in my son's voice? Absolute madness!'

'But that is precisely what happened, sire,' said the king's oldest and most trusted magician, Demetrius.

'This creature came and just attacked. We could not have been prepared, sire.'

The tall elderly man looked like any ordinary wizard. He had a tall, wide brimmed hat and a long, flowing beard that almost touched the ground. His skin was worn and wrinkled, but his eyes displayed a kind of youthful appearance. He had vowed to act as the king's advisor during these dark times.

'What in the Lord's name am I supposed to make of this?' The king held his hand to his head. 'Am I to believe that Fabian, my own flesh and blood – though I am loath to admit that he is mine – actually commanded a dragon to kidnap an ambassador of the Sinistrom? Sorry, but that sounds to me like an accusation, and an irrational one at that!'

'I don't believe for one second that the prince has anything to do with this deception, sire,' Demetrius said, raising the large mystical crook in his hand with much dramatic flair. 'There are indeed forces at work here, terrible and malevolent. I think we should all try to keep a cool head and not jump to conclusions.'

The king sat down again as he endeavoured to think about the accusation practically and logically.

'Obviously, it was a ruse of King Kardas's to kidnap his own son, and then pin the blame on me, but why? None of this makes the slightest bit of sense. Why the deception?' The councillors gave it some thought.

One said, stroking his beard meditatively:

'It is a subterfuge my lord. They obviously don't wish to draw first blood. Instead, they goad you into doing so. They make it appear that we kidnapped the Sinistrom heir, and they will inevitably send an army to force us into telling them where we have hidden their ambassador, in which instance one side will make a rash move. I fear we will be forced to show our hand, by which time all out war will seem like the only recourse.'

'Where is my son? I want him found. I want him found and brought to me. I want to get to the bottom of this situation right now.'

The councillor backed steadily away, leaving the room.

Tweak stood at the door to his old teacher's workshop. Demetrius was inside, resting after spending two hours in the presence of the king. The old wizard heard the knock at his door.

'Enter!'

The strange looking dwarf pushed the door open gently and stepped inside.

'It is I, Tweak,' he said, announcing himself at the threshold.

'Oh Tweak.' The Wizard barely moved as his old and frail body lay prostrate upon his daybed. 'Can't you see I'm resting? Yes?'

The old man sat upwards finally and let out a sigh.

Tweak stepped forwards.

'I need to know what to do,' he said. 'I witnessed something earlier, something that would make your hair stand on end and your hat stand upright.'

'What the devil are you talking about?' Demetrius asked, losing patients.

'Fabian,' the dwarf replied. 'I used the mirror of sight and it showed me something truly disturbing. I saw in the mirror's reflection our prince become a monster!'

'A monster?' the wizard said, putting on his spectacles. 'Well, let me say that you are not the first today to make a wild accusation like this. People all over the kingdom are saying that the prince is a dragon.' The old wizard snorted. 'Would be damned funny if it wasn't so inappropriate! And now you, Tweak. You believe this preposterous rumour?'

The old man began tut-tutting.

'And I suppose the mirror showed you our king as well turn into a magnificent butterfly to spirit King Kardas off into the yawning depths of hell?'

'Not exactly,' Tweak replied, looking at his old mentor as if the duffer was losing all perspective on things.

'Tweak, you should understand that that old mirror should be used sparingly. It is a relic and as such, decrepit. Don't believe everything you see in that mirror.'

'But, but, but…'

The wizard put up a hand to gesture that he had heard quite enough. He went and he lay down upon the daybed. His head rested on his soft pillow and he fell dreamily into a magical sleep.

Tweak stood by the doorway. None of his questions had been answered. But he knew he had to act and fast. The monster was still at large in the kingdom. Fabian had been witnessed returning.

Fabian had no idea where he had been or what had happened to him. Casting his eyes around the room in which he lay he noticed the stables and the silage, as well as the tools and implements propped against a beam. The sound of a horse drew his attention. How he got here, he did not know? The last he knew he was in the market place. He remembered saving a child from a horse that had been spooked.

'You.'

Fabian turned his head as he heard the voice behind him.

He recognised the dwarf standing by the stable doors.

'You monster,' the strange little man said in an accusing manner.

'Tweak?' Fabian looked understandably confused. 'What? What happened? What are you…?'

'Don't even try to act like you don't know,' said the dwarf, reproachfully.

'Don't know? Don't know what? Tweak, I really don't know what happened. First I was in the market and then I was—'

The dwarf interrupted:

'I saw what you did. I saw what you are. You're a monster. You're a demon!'

'What? Tweak, have you taken leave of your senses? What in the Lord's good name are you talking about? I'm not a monster.'

'No? Then how come you turned into one? How come you spirited the ambassador away, burning the entire market square with your dragon's fire? If you want evidence, I'll give you evidence!'

'What?' said the prince. 'Tør? What happened to him?'

The dwarf offered the prince a distrustful smile.

'You know full well where he is. It knows. That dragon. Your demonic alter ego. You turned into a big fire breathing dragon. You snatched him up. You took him. Now this kingdom could go to war for your actions. They all know what you did, you monster.'

Fabian had no idea how or why, but something came over him—a powerful and violent emotion. He heard a sound. It was a monstrous holler. He didn't know what was more disturbing, the sound itself or the fact that it had come from his own mouth. Perhaps there was something in what Tweak had said after all. In a trice, the young man found himself before the hapless dwarf, on all fours, baying like an animal. The dwarf turned quickly and ran from the barn. Fabian had no idea what had come over him. He sat, stunned. Voices were coming from outside the barn.

'He's in there.' He heard Tweak's shouts.

Without thinking, Fabian stood up. He looked around. His horse was peering at him over the stable gate. Fabian wasted little time. He opened the gate and leapt onto the creature's back. Digging his heals into the creature's flank the horse bolted for the doors.

The two alerted soldiers and Tweak darted away suddenly as the animal darted full pelt between them and out across the open courtyard.

The order was given to lower the portcullis, though not nearly fast enough to prevent the flight of the prince.

Beyond the confines of the city lay the enemy encampments. Fabian brought his steed to a halt. He couldn't go forwards. If it was correct what Tweak had told him, then the armies of the Sinistrom would certainly take him captive. If he turned back he would be arrested for treason. He had to entertain the possibility that he was a fugitive on the run. There was really only one route of escape—through the forest. That seemed to be the only spot the hordes of the Sinistrom did not occupy. Digging his heals in, he steered the animal in the direction of the trees to the left. Beyond this place he would be safe. He would keep riding. He looked over his shoulder. In the distance he saw the citadel and the life he was leaving behind.

The forest was dense so he decided to make the rest of the journey on foot. He led his horse through the thicket. It took him an hour, but eventually he crossed to the other side. So this is what it looked like, the world beyond the bounds of his father's kingdom. He witnessed the fire that still burned a trail cross country.

If there was the slightest possibility that there had been an actual dragon then it was up to the prince to investigate it.

Dwelling for a moment on the implausible, Fabian recalled what he had read about dragons or, more to the point, dragon fire. It was very tricky to extinguish, and he remembered that it burned for days on end.

The king's men had not given chase. Instead they approached the enemy encampments with the offer of an appraisal. A momentary truce. They suggested to work together to bring back the renegade and force him to tell where he had hidden Tør.

It was agreed that a truce would be observed, and a small hunting party set out to track the escapee.

Tweak decided to do a bit of tracking by himself. He wandered into the forest, catching the recent scent of Fabian's cologne. The foot and hoof prints in the dirt gave away their flight, and Tweak understood all too well where Fabian had headed. He cast a spell of speed which enabled him to move with the momentum of a horse. His stubby little legs wobbled and vibrated like two stumpy harp strings. Then, with a mighty whoosh, his portly frame was propelled forwards at a rate of knots. To hear his sudden cry of surprise one might have thought that he had lost control of his legs entirely, but after a moment or two of finding them again, he began to shout with excitement as he picked up even more speed, kicking up a dust trail in his wake.

Chapter 6

Far beyond the kingdom of Mundor there existed many wonders. There were also some rural towns and territories, castles where simple people went about their daily lives oblivious to the highly advanced cultures that existed in the clouds above their heads.

In the fields where the barley grew the farmer stopped to wipe the sweat from his brow. Looking toward the sky he detected short, intermittent glints of light. Squinting his eyes, he tried to make out what these tiny polished items where. They were moving slowly at first and then began to dart around the clouds in strange patterns.

Too fast to be swifts or starlings, the farmer thought, puzzled. *What are they?*

Kardas waited, watching the drone probes on his viewer.

'We are getting no telemetry back,' said one of his technicians.

'This is the location, is it not?' asked Kardas. 'This is where the dragon first disappeared and then reappeared?'

'It is, sire. There is nothing here though. The drones detect nothing but a slight distortion.'

'A distortion?'

'Yes, sire. We detected a slight hazing affect behind a cloud in this vicinity. Could be anything. Could be atmospherics. Sun spots. Anything.'

'Allow the drones to remain another hour. They may pick up something else.'

'Yes, sire.'

Urban Cloud, a city of secrecy floating high above the arid tundra, opened its doors to the covert delegation of hooded Head Hunters. They acknowledged the small delegation of Viper Masters with a cool nod. The vipers reserved their own inflated sense of superiority. They knew that the Head Hunters were pirates and mercenaries. They did what they did for a price. They believed in nothing. But while Malecarjan continued to line their pockets the hunters could be trusted, for the time being anyway. One of the Viper Masters goaded Tør a little too roughly. The prisoner fell to the deck and pondered momentarily the chains linking his arms together, looking steadily and defiantly up at his captors. A trickle of blood stained the corner of Tør's mouth.

The Head Hunter, a tall and feral looking specimen, adorned with a long red cloak, bared his fangs at the prisoner.

'Pick that up,' he commanded his hunters. 'Take him to a cell. A cold, confined, unpleasant one.'

The Head Hunters did as they were told and hoisted the boy to his feet.

'I trust this intrusion you have brought to our door will not last?' asked the commanding Head Hunter, glaring at the lead Viper Master. 'Your powerful leaders have dispatched drones to try and ascertain where your ambassador has been taken.'

The Viper Masters exchanged concerned looks amongst each other.

'No need to worry,' said the Head Hunter. 'We are quite safe from probes here. All they will see is a phased distortion. As far as they know it's a perplexing mystery that bares scrutiny. That is until they grow tired of looking.'

The Head Hunters goaded Tør into an empty cell. There was no explanation as to why he had been sent here. The slam of the prison doors was the only answer he would likely receive.

The vast city of Urban Cloud had a central council chamber. The doors slid open to allow a red cloaked figure to enter. This was the ringleader, the pirate king himself. His name was Cougar Chuko.

Seated at the head of a long conference table, Malecarjan waited for his host to make his report. Somewhere near by, fists clenched in anger began to pound the walls. Yelled threats echoed throughout the small area known as the brig, though none of the guards seemed to take any notice. It was simply an annoyance that no one here could be bothered to prevent.

'If this prisoner you brought me keeps this up I'll eject him from Urban Cloud and make him fly home!' said the Head Hunter. Chuko swung round suddenly, bending over the conference table and reminded his client of his expenses. Malecarjan, his employer, unfolded his arms and unlatched a small pouch from his belt. He slid it across the table. Chuko caught it with hands too human to be paws, though far too stubby to be hands.

'You will do no such thing,' Malecarjan ordered. 'The ambassador is a guest here until this war is over.'

Cougar Chuko picked up the pouch of money and smiled, licking his fangs with delight.

'Your payment in full,' said the Viper Master. 'I wanted to make sure you keep up your end of the bargain. You have the technology and the discretion, qualities we require during this phase our plan. I pay extra for these singular assurances. I want no doubt in my mind that Tør will be kept here in secret until our final phase is complete. No disintegrations. Am I clear?'

'Clear as glass,' answered the Cougar with glee. 'Already we succeed in impeding endeavours by Kardass to locate the whereabouts of your ambassador. He will not find us. We are far more advanced than anything they can throw at us.'

Malecarjan strolled past the Head Hunter, marching into the corridor where a large window greeted him boasting full views of the skies above the planet. The clouds were slow moving, revealing only small flecks of blue beyond. They didn't call this city Urban Cloud for nothing. It was the technological mystery in a world of medieval castles and magical lands. It was massive. A giant metal behemoth of the heavens, it possessed an alien quality, automated and strictly controlled like a station, or a powerful mother ship. It was the single paradox to grace the skies of a primitive world. Yet here it existed.

Malecarjan's eyes burned red behind the iron recess grating in his visor, within the black void where a man's features might have been more flattering to behold.

'You stand to profit greatly from this venture,' he said. 'As do we all. Do not take my generosity for granted.'

'I don't,' replied Cougar, nervously.

'I will have my war,' Malecarjan muttered. 'I will have my world. Kardas and his family have their beauty, and condemned us, his creations, to darkness, servitude, and ugliness, ugliness which all men shun. No longer! For when this war is over the snakes shall live in the light and savour the beauty of sweet charm and know what it is to reign supreme.'

Cougar Chuko, standing in a shadow and rubbing his hands together with obsequious glee, coughed to obtain his client's full attention. Malecarjan did not turn from the view and merely replied,

'Yes? What is it you want?'

Chuko only smiled a toothy, deferential smile.

'I simply wish to convey our gratitude to one of our most illustrious customers and grant you a free benefit. On the house, as it were.'

Malecarjan did not turn around. He wasn't that interested in charity, to say nothing of Chuko's irritating, toadying nature.

'Oh?' he asked, placing his hands behind his back.

'Yes. We have a room here…'

'I would suspect you have many.'

The sarcasm was not lost on Chuko as he smiled.

'I realise that, sir…Please allow me to clarify.'

'Then explain quickly! I have little time to squander on gimmicks.'

'My lord, this particular room holds a power, an immense power. A force of supremacy of which you might want to take advantage.'

'I have no idea what it is you are talking about!'

Malecarjan's words sounded testy.

Cougar Chuko decided to take another approach.

'Would you like powers? A sample of what we can offer you, My Lord.'

Malecarjan turned and finally regarded the obsequious microbe standing before him.

'What kind of power?' Malecarjan asked.

'Real power,' the cougar answered, grinning. 'The power of the ancients. The power of the dragon within your veins. No extra cost. A sample, if you will. What do you say?'

This peaked Malecarjan's attention suddenly.

'Dragon's power?'

'Not just any dragons. Skylantern Dragons, your magnificence.'

'They were once the stuff of legend.' Malecarjan permitted himself the luxury of intrigue.

'Indeed. They were capable of bestowing great power upon those they deemed worthy.'

'And why are you bothering to tell me this? These Dragons are merely stories to entertain children. They do not exist.'

'Contrary to popular belief...' The Head Hunter explained: 'As it so happens, we certainly do have Skylanterns here and under our supervision.'

Chuko opened the palm of his hand to reveal a small aura of light, no larger than a marble. Malecarjan approached the light, his interest peaking suddenly.

'Impossible!' Malecarjan muttered.

'Not impossible, but attainable through unconventional channels. This could be yours, free of charge.'

'Tell me more!'

Chuko closed his fist, extinguishing the light within, and smiled again. He believed he had won his customer over at last.

'I'll do better. I'll show you. Follow me.'

Malecarjan felt his blood quicken. The Skylantern Dragons, according to the stories, were formidable creatures. Those who stood in their presence gleaned power for themselves and could wield magic, accomplish marvellous feats, do practically anything.

Malecarjan followed the Cougar to the lower level where, in a room that was protected by a lock, the dragons were cautioned to reside. Chuko entered the combination and the lock clicked open, at once making the contents of the storage room accessible. The large metal door swung open automatically.

The Head Hunter and his client both crossed the threshold.

To his astonishment, seven orbs were somewhat larger in stature to the one Chuko had previously held in his hand. Whereas that one was the size of a marble these were the size of a clenched fist. The globes stood atop seven pedestals.

'Behold the Skylantern Dragons. Imprisoned here for all time.'

'How is this possible?' Malecarjan asked, inspecting each orb as he stepped into the room.

'Great and powerful magic may not be overwhelmed by a lesser magic, only by science and technology. Here, great magic is imprisoned by science alone. A gift to you, my lord.'

'What do I do?'

'Simply stand in the centre and allow the orbs to fuel you. Remember, this boost is totally free. Further boosts will cost you. Enjoy!'

Backing out of the room, Chuko left his client to his own devices.

Malecarjan could see beyond each glorious light which the orbs emitted. He witnessed the dragons in their prisons, screaming to get out. Much of their power had been depleted in the course of profit and gain. Even Malecarjan felt sick to his stomach. However, it did not stop him from taking full advantage of the situation. He waited for a reaction. The orbs glowed brighter than before, and Malecarjan began to realise that something truly remarkable was about to happen.

One orb grew brighter than all the others. Nothing further happened for a moment, then a bolt of energy, a discharge, was passed from one dragon orb to another, then another. It was like a circuit of sorts. Each one passed the power to the next. The last orb fizzled and sparked. Malecarjan felt that this was somehow a trick, a Head Hunter ploy to destroy him, but no. Before Lord Malecarjan could do anything, the final orb bathed him in energy too potent to be recognised. Chuko had called it a boost. This was more than that. Plumes of energy generated by the captive dragons entered Malecarjan's muscular frame, satiating him with magic he had never felt in his entire existence.

The pulse of energy faded gently. As the orb's connections evaporated, Malecarjan merely stood silent, still watching the power, the fire, like an aura, enveloping his hands and traveling up his arms. Indeed, his entire body was engulfed. But it felt good! It felt powerful!

Chapter 7

The guard at the gate saw the horse in the distance approaching at a gallop. It was pouring with rain as night crept in.

Prince Fabian had spied the town, surrounded by a large stockade. Digging his heels into the flanks of his steed, he bid the creature go faster. Lightning flashed, followed some time later by a faint thunder crash. He came up to the wall and dismounted. A small peephole slid open revealing a pair of mean eyes.

'What's your purpose here?' bellowed the guard at the traveller.

'I'm a nomad from the kingdom of Mundor. I am only seeking shelter for the night. I have money.'

The prince did not wish to reveal his true identity. He was a wanted man. It would be better that they did not learn of his true purpose here.

'Sure, come in!'

The gates creaked open. Fabian, hoping to find a dry place to spend the night, mounted his horse and commanded the creature to advance past the stockade. It didn't take him long to find suitable stables, a room, and lastly a good hearty meal at one of the lodges in the centre of town.

The Laughing Duck was probably the most amusing name he had heard in reference to a tavern. It certainly had a happy atmosphere with plenty of ale and ample entertainments. Fools kept the patrons amused with clean as well as dirty jokes.

When Fabian entered the tavern he walked straight up to the bar where the innkeeper, a bulky, rotund, and jolly looking man greeted him with a hearty smile.

'Welcome stranger!' He beamed, placing a well polished pint glass on the bar's wooden surface. 'What can I do for you? Is it a drink and a hearty meal ye be needing? We 'ave only the finest wines from Abril Cann in our cellar as well as the leanest beef this side of Mundor! Or if you are looking for a room, we have two vacancies left!'

'Sounds fine, thank you. I'll have a room and a meal, please,' the prince said, feeling his stomach growl.

'Very good, sir! So that will be a meal and a room. Single? Double…? I bet you are a hit with the ladies, eh?' The innkeeper winked. 'Or if not, we have a selection of girls you may be interested in. No?'

Fabian wasn't sure if the innkeeper ran an inn or a brothel. The offer wasn't remotely tempting.

'Just a single room and a meal please.'

'Okay. Would that be for just one night?'

'Just one, thank you.'

'Good, good.'

The innkeeper wrote it all down on a piece of paper with a quill.

'What's the name, please?'

Fabian thought about the name. He needed a false name and fast.

'Smith,' he said. 'Mr. Smith.'

All right, so it probably wasn't the most imaginative choice, but it certainly did the trick.

'All right, Mr. Smith. If you'd take a table I'll get someone to bring you your meal when it's ready.'

Tweak had arrived at the town shortly after Fabian. He too had managed to find suitable lodgings for the night. It was perfect, commanding a clear view of the inn across the street. He had positioned a spy glass with a magnifying lens atop a wooden tripod and aimed it directly at Fabian's room. There was no light emanating from the window which meant that either Fabian was already sound asleep or that he was at the bar, enjoying the entertainments. Either way, there was very little for Tweak to do but kill some time before morning.

Perhaps a little light reading would help. The dwarf noticed that there was a single shelf with a selection of thick, leather bound books adorning it. He lifted one off and read the title. It was a book of local myths and legends. Tweak took the title and he went to lie on the bed. He opened the large cover and began to read. The first page told of mages and men that were capable of great power. He turned the page again. There were descriptions of trees that could cast spells and mushrooms that talked. In another section under the title, *Dangerous Places* he began to read an account given by a traveler who had lost a friend. He had lost him to an underground waterfall of all things. According to the passage, these dangerous and enchanted falls could trap anyone who entered them behind a wall of water. The waters would suddenly close in over the victim, leaving him trapped and alone to drown. Pale and frightened, Tweak looked up from the tome. He could not possibly conceive of a more terrifying way to die. He closed the book and shuffled from the bed. Perhaps it was true and ignorance was bliss.

* * *

Taking another look at the room there really didn't appear to be too many free tables left. There seemed to be a dozen or so and were all occupied. Fabian craned his neck, trying to see over the heads of people who were standing, talking. There was one table, right next to the fire at the back of the room, situated upon a landing. It was a large table, one that had only a single occupant.

Taking his leave of the innkeeper, he tried to squeeze by the crowds. People were loud and rowdy. This was probably not as congenial a respite as he had at first suspected, but the food smelled good and that was all he really wanted.

Prince Fabian began to notice there were a group of people sitting at a table who were looking at him. Some of them merely kept glancing at him. Others at intervals. A large man was swathed in a cloak and hood. He was the rudest. In spite of his appearance, he continued to hold Fabian in a cool and tacit scrutiny. Fabian looked him up and down nervously. The large stranger had the oddest face he had ever seen. His skin looked hard, jagged like stone.

The prince paid the stone man no more heed and simply turned his attentions to the person sat next to him. This one was cat-like and had fur. She kept checking him furtively from behind wisps of smoke that emanated from a cigarette holder of sorts. The creature appeared to be female, with large feline eyes, with a cat tail that suddenly craned upwards from the concealment of a short leather skirt.

Feeling a little bit like the outsider and sensing the irony in his vulgar behavior, Fabian chose not to keep staring.

Just a short distance from the inn was the old church grounds. At night it was a very foreboding place to enter, particularly the mausoleum with its ground vapours and tombstones depicting monsters and gargoyles of every description. You see, the people in this corner of the world had a ritual which was centered around a belief that anyone who had committed a serious crime in life should not, under any circumstances, be buried in the same grounds as the innocent. And this cemetery was a place in which people had been burying their violent criminals for years.

One such mausoleum was the burial place of the vampire known to many in these parts as Shollom Vi'shiid. In life he was a great magician until one day he decided to follow the dark arts and discovered that the way to reap men's souls was through their dreams. But each man had but one soul to give him. Many years ago, he had fed himself richly on the essences of every creature in the town, gorging himself like a parasite upon the weak and unsuspecting alike. That was until the day the remaining town's folk who had not been fed upon decided to band together and take charge of the matter. To cut a very long story short, Shollom Vi'shiid was buried alive for his crimes. Crimes that, strangely though this may sound, continued to be committed once in every blue moon.

That night there was just such a moon: full and blue. Stone scraped upon stone as the great mausoleum door slowly opened.

In the kitchen, the chef mustered up a meal for the patrons of the inn. He was busy stirring up a mixture of herbs with mortar and pestle. He stopped suddenly, feeling the room rapidly dropping in temperature. He knew his master was coming. The pupils of his eyes quickly drained of colour, as did the pigmentation of his skin. At this point the inn keeper entered the kitchen, joining the chef. Both men had been swayed by the evil in this town. Both men unfortunately had succumbed to the evil that was about to make an appearance.

'They are here,' he said in a subdued voice. 'Seven new strangers.'

The transparent entity appeared like a white vapour that undulated and swelled. That evil had made its sudden entry. The kitchen turned cold, as cold as hell, and as prisoners the chef and inn keeper were in thrall to the approaching evil.

'Take him his meal,' the voice from the entity commanded in a low raspy tone, 'and then I shall relish mine.'

The chef emptied a bottle of a strange blue liquid over the meal, and then handed the plate to the inn keeper.

In the tavern, Fabian waited patiently.

A troop of acrobats and fools kept the patrons entertained on the stage. Two actors, a small man and a fat woman argued, busy enacting marital bliss, while a fool, busy trying to cheer the pair up, was tripping over his own feet and generally making a nuisance of himself. The crowd laughed.

Fabian was handed his meal. Tears were rolling down his eyes through watching the spectacle. He couldn't remember when he had laughed so much.

After the entertainers had ended and once Fabian had finished his meal, and polished off a few glasses of house wine, he retired to his room. He was starting to feel a little light headed. He managed to get his key in the lock. Flinging the door wide, he staggered in. Not bothering to undress, he collapsed on the bed. The ceiling spun round in that usual nauseating fashion, so much so he clenched his eyes shut to stop his stomach from churning too much.

Back inside the bar the stone man looked round at the feline woman sitting next to him, nodded, and then rose, moving over to the window where another tall being sat, holding a device much like a computer pad.

'Was that Fabian?' the tall man asked. 'Have you identified him yet?'

The stone man nodded silently.

'Then it would be a good time for our man to show his full colours. Send word to the others. We make a move tonight.'

Chapter 8

Fabian dreamt of his own comfortable quarters back home. He imagined the room where he used to sleep as a child. His mother would sit on the corner of the bed and tell him stories. He missed his mother dearly, especially in times such as these when he was all alone. Back home, he kept a small framed portrait of his mother by his bedside, a reminder that he was loved. He thought of her more and more as time endeavoured to replace her dear memory with his father's brutish nature. Though Prince Fabian held on to the belief that this woman who had once been a major part of his life was somehow watching him from someplace distant, guiding him, and making him strong.

He dreamt of when he was just 14 years of age. It was the day his mother took him on the hunt. She was a tall, handsome woman dressed in a leather tunic with a sash of crimson and sporting a sword that was sheathed at her side. She looked at her 14 year-old son and smiled with pride to see her only child mounting a horse, looking every bit the man she suspected he'd one day become. She had given the boy a sword on his 14th birthday. It was small and lightly weighted, just right for a boy his age. He had practiced with it every day since. This was going to be his first hunt. It was best he came prepared.

The land was blanketed in snow. The wind was cold as the trodden earth. In the distance, Prince Fabian could see the mountain range, snow capped and full of peril. But he was safe. His mother was present. Mr. Cosgrove, the King's hunter and tracker, accompanied them. He was an old man, but he knew the wild lands like the back of his hand. He had brought his trusty sidearm and a large hunting knife. He would need his weapons as well as his wits. It had been said that a number of large predators had previously come down from their dwellings to find food in the valley near Mundor and taken flight with a number of livestock.

'Are you ready, son?' asked the queen, her eyes flashing with passion.

'You bet!' the 14 year old boy answered with a surge of excitement.

The queen jabbed her stirrups into the flanks of her mount, and Fabian watched as the beast charged off.

'Yah! Yah!' the boy shouted, goading his steed.

Hunting upon his father's ancestral lands was an

adventure, though quests and excitement came quite freely in those days. King René was carefree and the boy prince was a contented soul.

The prince was not afraid of the wolves at first. In truth, he'd never seen one. His mother had told him stories, grizzly yarns that only served to pique the youngster's imagination and fill him with enthusiasm for the hunt. And this was his first.

As the two approached the mountain, Fabian noticed a strange conglomeration of metal and wires peeking out of the snow. When he asked what it was Mr. Cosgrove simply replied that it was a remnant from a time long ago, from a period before the great transformation of the world. The boy slowed his horse to take a closer look.

'What is it for?'

Nobody could say.

'Our history is something long forgotten,' she said. 'It is unknown what these things were used for. They are but relics of an age now completely alien to us.'

She bid her son to move on. The sooner they reached their quarry, the sooner they could go home.

They cantered for a quarter of an hour up those steep rises before hearing the telltale sign of howling. Though there were no visible signs of wolves, not yet. The boy looked a little more concerned as he rode, seeing the snow and no tracks but their own. The tall trees and conifers around them could have hidden a multitude of massacres. And little did either of them realise that they too were being hunted.

Heavy panting peppered the air around them. Then foot falls began to follow. More panting. Snarling. The young prince panicked, digging into the flanks of his steed. He went galloping past as his mother shouted to her son, telling him not to panic.

She galloped after him with her musket primed. Mr. Cosgrove paused for only a moment and pressed on, matching the speed of his queen. Something was not right. The wolves were tricky. He knew those animals well. But he was beginning to get the impression that whatever was out there was something far more dangerous.

The Queen was further up ahead.

What happened next caused her blood to freeze and the hair to rise on the back of her neck. Fabian's horse reared, hurling the boy from its back. His sword too was thrown in the fall. This creature that had excited such sudden panic was no ordinary wolf. It was a riding wolf, twice the size of any animal she had previously seen in these woods. Nearly the size of a horse, the wolf had its eye on Fabian. Fabian looked up, nursing his head, and saw it as it trod towards him, slowly, its massive fangs bared. He looked anxiously about him. His weapon, the sword his mother had given him as a present was nowhere to be seen. Fabian's heart knocked in his young breast.

The queen held her musket steady and fired a shot. The vicious creature collapsed to the ground, turning the snow a deep red.

'Mother!' the boy screamed out a warning.

Too late. Another beast launched itself at the woman, knocking her from her steed, the musket tumbling out of her hands.

He looked about him, desperately searching for signs of Mr. Cosgrove. Only his steed was visible several yards off. The large majestic creature was alone. No signs at all of the old man.

Another large wolf came in from the opposite direction, stalking the queen, its fangs tingling with the thought of the kill.

'Mother, no!' he shouted again. This was something no child needed to see, his own mother being mauled and carried off by wild vermin such as these. And it had all happened so quickly.

They were going to come after him next. The boy shivered with the cold and fear. Three more creatures trod slowly from either side, knowing that they had the child cornered. One of the wolves snarled and bayed as the boy closed his eyes tightly. The sound of a gun shot opened them again. He looked around. The wolf howled in pain. It had fallen. A second and a third shot made sure the others fled in panic. The boy looked round again. Mr. Cosgrove's horse was still standing and there, lying upon the earth was Mr. Cosgrove himself. Fabian recognised the shape. He rose to his feet, running in the direction of the man who had saved his life. As he approached he could see Mr. Cosgrove had been badly injured. One of those creatures must have knocked him from his horse. A fight ensued with the old man proving to be the victor. However, judging by the amount of blood he was loosing perhaps the word 'victor' was a little too optimistic.

'My boy,' he said in a faint voice as he looked up at the little face staring tearfully down at him. 'I couldn't save your mother in time. Forgive…'

His words trailed off. Fabian watched, horrified at the sight of the old man's appearance. It was a sight he never forgot: the look of Mr. Cosgrove. The sudden lifelessness of his eyes as they continued to stare upwards towards the sky. His life blood stained the area widely upon which he lay.

The 14 year-old boy, unresponsive for a time, shivered and finally gave out a loud scream of confusion and pain and terror which steadily decreased to a whimper.

What now? Go back alone? Gather the horses and tell the king of the tragic news? Little did the boy realize just how his father would react to this report. Little did he know how much of a coward the father would make him feel for not standing up to the wolves. After all, these were not your average class of wolf. These were enchanted predators, creatures born more of a dark magic than of the wilderness. And those who had not witnessed this attack were destined never to believe the ravings of a boy.

The stars stared downwards to the vast snowy tundra and blinked indifferently as they always had, and would do for many, many years to come. Freedom was swept away, along with happiness, and sadness took its icy grip over René's kingdom, turning bitterness and blame and hardening it into something worse.

But the face of that wolf haunted Fabian even in his dreams.

Over his dream state, looming high like a wraith above his bed materialized a robed figure. Forbidding and ghoul-like, the creature gestured with a translucent, depressed hand, the fingers tapering into sharp, chipped and hewn points. Shollom Vi'shiid, the master soul drinker. It was he all along who had been influencing Fabian's dreams, bringing memories long buried to the fore. Shollom uttered a mantra in a cracked and whispered tone, its clawed, almost sallow hand motioning at the boy, trying to force the dreams upon its sleeping victim.

The face of the victim, still trapped in the reverie, tossed from side to side, sternly trying to shake the vision.

Fiercely, the victim awoke. Teeth clenched and perspiration clinging to his brow, Prince Fabian tried to gain control of his faculties to protect himself from the intruder.

Shollom clenched his fist suddenly and more nightmares came flooding in to assault Fabian's mind. Pressing his head back into the pillow, Fabian looked like he was having a seizure. He was unprepared for the sheer barrage of images that were at that moment flooding into his brain. His teeth clenched tightly as he forced his fists shut, contracting with the entourage of terror and imagery.

'You killed your mother. You watched her die.'

He could hear these words in his head being spoken over and over.

'You did nothing. You are a coward. You are a freak. You let her die.'

'No. No!'

The sound that he uttered from his lips suddenly was like an abrupt and unexpected wake up call. His eyes opened in a flash, though they were bright emerald and nictitating, appearing reptilian. Then the vermillion tincture formed, burning like a raging, cursing fire. The creature that dwelled within the depths of his skin was waking. His body mass suddenly increased as he grew talons from his fingers and toes. Jade coloured scales rippled from his flesh this time, flipping and turning like a pack of playing cards falling back to back. The human pelt was replaced quickly with many tiny, hard protective plates and blazing with magnificence. Shollom Vi'shiid hesitated for a moment and looked on as his powers were inverted suddenly, rebounding back on him.

The Prince was yet again The Dragon Tolan, too powerful for the ghost that tried desperately to regain control. In this form, the Dragon Tolan prince could not be coerced or overcome.

A brief but sonorous thunder roar from the

transformed prince soon got the evil Shollom Vi'shiid scrambling for safety. He seeped through a solid wall as though it were made of air. The Dragon Tolan smashed straight through the outside wall, flexing its webbed wings, taking flight after the wraith that had attacked him.

In the narrow street, flanked with white washed walls and wooden beams, the stone man – that same strange individual Fabian had seen earlier on in the tavern – stood with a couple of his companions watching the destruction. They looked as though they too wanted a piece of the action, the way they appeared primed to attack.

The Dragon Tolan filled the sky with fire as the cowardly wraith fled. Once this menace had vanished with terror the Dragon Tolan circled once, before settling in the center of the town. Its size began to decrease as it turned. From scaly skin into soft human flesh, the dragon once again became a man. The young prince fell to his knees. He looked up to witness several unusual faces peering down at him. Six beings of uncommon appearance…Six faces of untold origin. Were they mutants or the men of old his mother had told him about? One of them, a tall hulk of a man whose entire face and body was composed of stone stepped forward.

'He is truly powerful as was foretold,' the stone man said.

'Yes,' another individual replied. This person was a female with spikes protruding from her pale, metallic skin. 'And he knows what trouble brews in the Northlands. He should be able to tell us of the private wars as brooked by our most ancient enemies.'

Someone else had witnessed the disturbance from a hidden location in the town. Tweak had been observing from a discreet place of hiding, though he could barely believe his eyes. What evil was it that allowed the prince to not only become a dragon, but also to select a different skin pigmentation? Also the shape of the dragon, the very physical nature of the great beast was different this time. Whereas before the creature was red and more bipedal in appearance, this latest iteration was more like a reptile, and had jade skin.

Indeed some kind of strategy was needed.

Chapter 9

Prince Fabian was helped to his feet by the man with the stone face.

'Welcome stranger, Dragon Tolan,' one of the outsiders said with a friendly voice.

The stranger had a hood that covered most of his head. The little that could be seen of his face had a tattoo of a feathered creature, a bird that encompassed the left hemisphere of his face.

'Who are you? What do you want from me?' the prince asked.

'I am Justas Marl,' the tall figure replied, and instantly the tattoo on his face began to become animate, turning into a distinct being. The small bird flew from the man's face, circled the narrow street just once, then returned, merging again with the face of the one who had called himself Justas Marl. That was some kind of enchanted tattoo!

The stone man stepped forwards with a low, thunderous traipse. Lifting his stone hand, he introduced himself as Draethor, the Man of Stone. Gingerly, Fabian raised his hand and placed it squarely in the not so inconsiderate palm of the stone man.

A sleek feminine feline leapt up onto a stone bench and introduced herself as Katt Brutal, smiling cheekily.

'Hey,' she said and began to slide her tongue along her fur in that way cats do when grooming.

Another stranger stepped forwards. This one was taller and appeared to have amour covered in metal spikes. Even her head had a curious metallic shine to it. She seemed bulkier than her feline friend. Iron May was her name.

'You are undisciplined in the ways of magic.'

The others cast her looks as she spoke. Her honesty notwithstanding, the man they called Colonel Warclaw grunted. This man, this creature, held the likeness of a crab with his hard, armored skin and metal claws. He decided to cut the prince some slack by saying:

'Don't worry, kid. As far as I'm concerned you definitely nailed it. Why, that old wraith beat a retreat so fast you'd have thought the plague was back in town.' And he laughed a hearty laugh.

The Prince looked up. From where he stood he could plainly see the destruction. There was fire raging atop one of the buildings, and a dragon-shaped hole carved into the side of the inn.

'What? What happened?' the prince felt a sudden pang of uneasiness. 'The dragon. Was it here?'

Fabian could barely believe his eyes. He appeared mortified.

'You could say that, yes?' Draethor said, rubbing his head.

'You look surprised' Marl noticed.

'I don't remember a dragon,' Fabian replied. 'I don't remember—? What am I doing here? Will somebody kindly explain what happened?'

All the strangers that had gathered looked at each other and then returned their gazes to the prince.

It was Marl who attempted to explain:

'You don't know. You have no idea of the power you command as The Dragon Tolan? But surly you feel its presence when it comes upon you, when it changes? The changes your body goes through whenever the power of the dragon is revealed? My young friend, you are the Dragon Tolan.'

Fabian looked down at his hands. This epiphany sent a sudden shudder down his spine as he remembered the moment in the forest. The baffling event that saved him from the pitcher plant and had left him unconscious in the woods. He assumed it had been the king's men who rescued him from the maw. And Tweak had made strange accusations in the stables before he left. He spoke of a dragon, a demon that appeared like a destructive alter ego. This realisation wrought feelings of anxiety, then doubt, as the conclusion became clear: could he really have been responsible for the Ambassador's abduction?

The man's legs gave way. He collapsed and continued to sit as his mind ventured to make sense out of everything.

Another one of the strangers, a creature known as Centorionn, trotted to Fabian's side. The creature looked strange, though no stranger than his companions. Centorionn's body was segregated. The upper torso and head had the appearance of a human male while the lower half was that of a horse. He said to the prince in a mild voice:

'Fear not, my young dragon. Until you master the magic within, you may not understand that the power is at first primal. You must learn to master the form of the Dragon Tolan. Only then will you be able to attack your opponent without the fear of collateral damage.'

'Who are you people?' Fabian asked.

'We are like nomads.' The one with the odd tattoo

on his face answered with certainty. 'We are free men. We ask so little of man, and he in turn asks so very little of us.'

'I'm starting to get the feeling you know more about this dragon business than I do myself. You speak of magic, but all I know about it is that I'm cursed, blighted with some unknown witchcraft.'

Justas Marl could see the agitation build in the young prince's soul.

'Blighted? No. Gifted? Why, certainly. And through sight and meditation we, that is the brotherhood of mages, have become aware of these powerful gifts that you embody. We simply wish to help you understand.'

'Help me?' the boy interrupted. 'Why would you want to help me?'

'Because you are one of us,' the stone man answered. Fabian looked at him and wondered what in the heavens he could possibly have in common with a talking lump of rock.

'And because we need your help...' Justas Marl added, 'to restore the balance. A great and powerful enemy has risen in force and is systematically taking over the kingdoms of this dimension. They have a terrible weapon. Men of old used to call this weapon science until it was obliterated by magic.'

'You mean Sinistrom? I know they are presently in accord with my people. But they are not enemies!' Fabian protested.

'Some may not be enemies. Some maybe honourable. Others amidst their ranks are perhaps not as trustworthy,' said Justas Marl. 'In visions and in meditations I have seen vague intimations of future and present events as they will no doubt unfold. But as always the waters are murky and it is hard to see the bigger picture. But I have seen enough to be wary of your current "friends."'

'The Mecha Villeforms were ordered to stand down,' said the prince finally. Concern for Marl's warnings had got him to loosen his tongue.

'Ordered yes, but I would not trust them.'

Marl looked intently at the young prince. He was a man of learning, but more accurately, he was a man of experience.

He went on to explain. 'All true monsters have sight, but not the courage to turn both eyes to positive action. They see entitlement as something to be taken, by force if necessary. The truest monster is bitter frustration. It is the ego twisted and warped all out of serious proportion. All higher brain functions operate in the subterranean earth. That is what makes monsters slayers and men so monstrous.'

The young man stepped thoughtfully away from the seven strangers. Compelled to reflect, he thought of his beautiful emissary of peace, Tør. Was the creature, this dragon, evil? Was it responsible for Tør's disappearance?

'I suppose,' began Iron May in the throws of contemplation, 'there is only one question left that has not been raised…'

They all looked in May's direction as the metal plated mage looked directly at Prince Fabian.

'Why are you here? What could possibly have been so important that you leave your father's side while the enemy stands at your gates?'

'I am not a coward if that's what you are implying,' said the young man defensively.

'I am not implying anything. I am merely asking why.'

Fabian seemed unwilling to tell May the truth since they hardly knew each other, and quite frankly none of these mages had any reason to pry into his dealings anyway. They did appear to know about his curse and they did know a lot about the Sinistrom. Perhaps they were mercenaries for hire or maybe they had a grudge against the Sinistrom.

Marl looked at Fabian and smiled.

'I know the answer to that,' he told May as he maintained eye contact with the young prince. 'You are in love. And that love is the source of great sadness. I can see it in your eyes, Fabian. That is why you came. Your love, your feelings of guilt, it bears the seed of struggle, of a wanderlust in all the lonely niches of the world.'

'You know?' the prince said nervously.

'Know what?' asked Marl.

'My people are saying that the Sinistrom Ambassador was taken by a dragon. But I could not have done it, I tell you! It wasn't me. I would never do such a thing.'

'Then by the elimination of possibilities what we are left with must be the truth,' Marl proposed. 'I reason that what we maybe dealing with here is a powerful mage or shapeshifter, a trickster, someone capable of discrediting you and your alter ego. But why? That is the question. We might be seeing the finer strands to a much larger web of deceit and treachery.'

Fabian looked down at his hands again and steadily, contemplatively, he raised his eyes to meet Marl's.

'You are not the guilty party.' Marl avowed. 'This is my experience and my good sense informing me that you, my young friend, are innocent.'

'So, what are you saying?' asked Fabian, confused. 'That this shape changer came to the market looking like my dragon form and simply carried the ambassador off, just to discredit me?'

That sounded even more fanciful and ludicrous than the idea that a real dragon had come and snatched the envoiy for those same reasons.

'He may not be the guilty one here,' said May. 'He is hiding something—an emotion he does not want anyone to know about. He is ashamed and afraid of something.'

'Don't be impolite,' Marl advised his colleague in a measured tone. 'But you are correct in your assessment, May.'

Marl looked more fixedly into the young prince's eyes.

'Love brought you here. Love and only love was your soul motive. We may not be able to recognise the motives of our enemies quite yet, but I am standing here now and I can clearly see the motives of a young man who is, after all, young.'

'I came here to find the ambassador,' the prince stammered warily, looking directly at May. He was trying to measure her and Marl's eyes, seeing if they knew the truth or not.

'I followed the trail of destruction and…'

Marl offered a knowing smile.

'So, you came looking for the ambassador?'

'No! Yes, I mean…'

'Don't worry, my young friend.' Eased Marl, holding

his hands up in front of him. 'I was young once. You don't have to hide your feelings around me.'

'Wha-what?' The prince hesitated.

'Do you not have feelings for the ambassador?' Iron May asked, impersonally.

'That is none of your business!' he snapped, putting on a masculine voice that made him appear rather comical. Standing tall finally, he looked his accuser in the eye and said:

'Try not to pry into everything I do.'

'Be not ashamed' Marl said. 'There is no ignominy in tender feelings for another.'

The prince looked astounded that any man would speak thus. He turned his face away sheepishly, looking out across the town, seeing the flames that were consuming the building in the distance. It puzzled him that none of the town's folk had come out of their houses to see what the commotion had been. A dragon emerging from the side of a building, leaving a crater in the wall the size of a large fire breathing reptile and a blaze that had taken a whole residence, would have woken a whole city square. Where were the people? Where were the crowds?

* * *

Tweak in the meantime was staring out the window. He sat on a tall stool with his powerful magnifying lens in front of him and had witnessed Fabian and several odd looking people talking.

'Ah!' he said to himself, 'the game is once again afoot.'

Packing away his telescopic lens, he removed his fat little posterior from his stool and dashed towards the door. He would follow them. No doubt Fabian and his new friends were all in this criminal venture together

Fabian tilted his head, observing a lone figure sitting upon a balcony. A woman or a girl? She was too far away to tell. But this was the first he had seen anybody since this whole incident arose, not counting the six strangers he had just met. Turning his head again, he noticed a man leaning against a wooden strut supporting a large portico. This figure was alone too. Just standing still like a manikin. How very odd, thought Fabian.

'Look.' May began to point in the direction of the inn's side door.

They all turned their heads.

There, standing like a lifeless ghost, was the chef and the Innkeeper.

Before long, Fabian and the six strangers noticed more people as they emerged. Some moved slowly, advancing, filling the air with an eerie, unnatural groan.

'What? What is wrong with them?' asked Fabian.

'Look at their faces,' May said.

'Their eyes. Aye, dead as a cadaver's eyes.' Added Draethor.

'I think this is a town-wide full on possession,' Marl said. 'It's a goddamn epidemic!'

'What happened to them?' Fabian looked at the faces of the men and women that were slowly advancing on foot. They looked just as Draethor had described: like animated corpses.

'Look.' The prince pointed. 'There. That is one of the fools who entertained us on stage. Why do they all look like that?'

'They are bewitched,' said Marl. 'This is evil magic. Their minds have been turned. Though their appearance is fairly recent. This is no artifice or trickery. I don't think they want us to leave.'

Marionettes of the foul Shollom Vi'shiid, they stood at the fence surrounding the town. Farming implements and other household appliances in hand, they barred all departure exits.

'There's too many of them!' Fabian stammered.

'Damn!' said Draethor, grumpily. 'This is all I need! Thes creeps freak me the hell out. I knew I shouldn't have gotten out of my quarry bed this morning.'

'Get behind me, boy!' Iron May ordered, taking her place before the prince, shielding him from approaching harm.

Eerily, the people moved in for the attack. A low guttural hum, like a cacophony of moans, filled the air around them. The attackers measured their movements, though were decisive in their assaults. One or two made the first push against the six strangers and the prince. All Draethor had to do was lunge forward, carrying his hulk-like weight and caught a few of the cadavers in a head on collision.

Some of the other attackers were distracted by Marl's bird tattoo as it darted from his face, circled and made a decisive run on the people below. It perched on the shiny head of one man and continued to peck at his dome.

More hostilities followed. There was the inn keeper and his chef, neither of them seemed to respond to the sensibilities of those they were compelled to harm. They had one function and one function only: to kill the outsiders.

These were all innocent people once. Fabian couldn't

help but be aware of this troubling fact as he watched Marl, Colonel Warclaw and the others dismember a few of them without a second thought. He kept telling himself that it was all done in self defence, a truly despicable excuse to be certain.

Fabian suddenly noticed a little girl with a teddy bear gently and cautiously easing her tiny head round the porch of her parents' house. She was calling to her mother and father. Though no one seemed to notice or care all that much. Did the girl even realise that maybe her parents were bewitched? Taken hostage, body and soul, by the ghost that had them all in its terrible power?

The girl ran down the wooden steps and entered the town centre, still calling out for her parents.

At that moment, one of the zombies turned and scrutinized the child with a cold, unfeeling gaze.

'No!' Fabian shouted from behind Iron May. He rushed for the child as May turned and ordered the prince to return to her side. Fabian did not listen. He ran, gathering the little girl in his arms and carried her to safety.

'This is going well,' said May, ironically. 'First we find the individual we were looking for, and then find out he has no idea how to listen, and now we're about to be eaten by zombies! Can this day have started any better than it already has?'

Fabian tried to shield the child from the horror that was evident all around. He pressed her face against his chest, keeping her from seeing the terrible creatures that presented themselves like rodents in a clamour for blood. He said calming things to her while he held her close. As he glanced over his shoulder he didn't see the drained look in the eyes of the child, that death look which her kinsmen shared at that moment. She looked down at the exposed flesh of Fabian's arm and instantly went for it. Her teeth were at once sharp, jagged, and her skin was as sallow as a corpse.

Fabian noticed her sudden attack just in time. It was reflex more than anything. He simply kicked the child away, sending up dust and gravel as he did so. He had never hurt a child in his life and his sudden reaction both saddened and terrified him all at once. He sat there on the ground and watched the girl rise up before him. Would he have to kill her too? The thought disgusted him. He took to his feet and ran for the assembled mages. Clearly they were outnumbered.

Colonel Warclaw, armed with the exoskeleton of

a Bore Scorpion, took his Sabre of Many Talons and snatched one of the zombies, breaking the creature's skull with one tight squeeze.

Iron May slammed her shield cuffs into the gullet of another one of the attackers, bringing her knee guards up between its legs. Her cuffs as well as the shield guards had six-inch metal spikes that easily pierced necrotic flesh.

The mages were being goaded towards the stockade at the perimeter of the city. In the distance, a surge of confusion ensued as the attackers turned to witness what was coming up from behind.

The earth shook. A massive quake turned all attentions to the unseen epicentre.

A new danger…? They could not see for the heaving bodies, but there was something large bringing up the rear.

Mounds and mounds of clay rose up suddenly like a river of volcanic ash. There were shouts. There were raucous moans. Finally, the world seemed to ingest the unsuspecting townsfolk with a grand and conclusive mouthful. The remaining attackers stopped what they were doing and watched with deathlike eyes. They were unable to comprehend what had materialised. The earth had come to swallow the town's people, like a giant maw. It was as though a living graveyard had come to reclaim the animate dead.

Only the six strangers and a dozen or so more of the attackers remained. Silenced and numbed by what they had just seen. And again the earth rose, higher than before. Piles of weed, excretions of soil, tree root, and gravel towered upwards like a huge aperture, and then the earth plunged like aggressive serpents upon the wicked below. The earth had taken them in and none came back out again.

As the dust began to settle, Fabian and the strangers noted the sudden calm and stillness and the town without occupants. The zombies, making up a terrifying percentage of the population of this small town, had been inextricably taken.

One attacker was left however—the child with the teddy. She flailed her limbs awkwardly, her feet strutting to and fro inelegantly as, with fury, she screamed and retched at the unknown elements that had taken her kind. Her eyes were tiny and vicious. Her mouth, filled with chiselled, dishevelled teeth, foamed and frothed and was twisted into a tightened grimace. She looked at the strangers that were left standing and, with a rabid expression, spat at her hated enemies. She didn't notice the trees and vines coming up out of the ground behind her, not at first.

She hawked at the mages, expelling vile excretions from her mouth. The animosity in her eyes was in no way any indication of her true emotional state, a mood that was more to do with the puppeteer than the poor child that was being controlled, if indeed there was anything left of the child's true emotional state. Even her eyes, said to be the windows of the soul, did not appear to cry out for help in any way, shape, or form. She was completely taken over. But the puppeteer was unaware of the approaching danger.

The strangers watched, unable to intervene. This new terror, it came upon the child marionette. With vines of restraining greenery and thorny limbs the forces at work snatched the tiny girl without any warning. Tree roots, gnarled and tough, seized her arms and wrapped themselves round her neck. Tree sap oozed from the roots, from the capillaries. More of it issued, seeping out everywhere. The girl struggled. The ochre sap licked her arms and trickled down her legs. There was a loud but transitory cry as the stuff moved over her head, bleeding over her eyes, nose, and then her mouth. Cruel though it seemed, the sap hardened and she was caught like an insect in amber. The girl was instantly pulled back down into the earth with the rest of her kith and kin, never to be seen again.

Fabian felt his stomach turn. He span round quickly, choking up the remnants of the previous night's meal, realising that it had been cooked and prepared by these dreadful, though unfortunate creatures.

All at once the soul of the town fell to silence and desolation. Even the church bell had ceased its chime. It felt like the buildings had remained like this for years, mute as the grave, still as the untouched sepulchres left rotting in the quiet corners of the earth.

Out of the silence came a sound, like the rustle of wind through tall trees. Two strange looking beings materialised, emerging slowly from the disturbed soil. Once they had surface, they began to walk upright. Their faces were carved in wood and were framed, not by beards, but by moss and tiny leaves. Both of them approached the mages, and both had their hands extended in friendship.

'Who are you?' asked Fabian, looking at them strangely.

'Why, don't you recognise a couple of elemental mages when you see them?' Justas Marl replied, extending his hand to greet his old friends.

'Elemental mages…?'

'Aye,' said Marl. 'Elemental Mages are magicians that use the natural elements and all that you see and use it for good.'

The tall, tree-like man introduced himself as Treebon. The other presented himself as the elemental, A-Sap.

Treebon shook Marl's hand. Tiny insects and creatures scurried into the furrows of the creature's bark-like skin. The top of his head was like a sawn-off stump with a minuscule leaf that seemed to grow out of it like a human hair. A-Sap's skin on the other hand was covered in a thicket of fern and flower. His head was shaded by a bright red toadstool, adorning his crown like a wide brimmed hat.

Both these elementals had their own unique powers, Marl explained to Fabian. For example, Treebon had the ability to raise the earth, and A-Sap had the capability to encase evil doers in hard amber.

'So, to what do I owe the pleasure?' asked Marl, curiously. 'What brings you generally harmless gentlemen out here to these dark and dangerous places?'

'We heard about a disturbance,' replied Treebon. 'We sensed the return of our ancient enemy.'

'You mean the dragon?' Marl asked.

Treebon regarded his friend A-Sap. They both exchanged looks before giving an answer.

'We barely believed the stories we heard. We thought we had seen the last of them but then seeing is believing.'

'You have seen a real dragon?' Fabian enquired, starting to wonder at how old these two elemental mages were.

'Once,' replied the one called Treebon, 'many thousands of years ago, dragons lived in these valleys. Of cause, back then, men lived in vast cities and dwelled in huge buildings that reached the very sky and firmament. It was an era of technology and dragons. Back then, man and dragon lived in harmony, and both man and dragon were our mortal enemy. They cleared entire forests in a bid to expand their territory. Cities rose like huge glass monstrosities and pollution raged throughout the land.'

Fabian was at that very moment filled with a desire to hear more. He had never encountered anyone who had lived for over a thousand years. This was a rare and unexpected opportunity to find out about this world's buried history. But there were further pressing issues at hand.

The tree continued:

'Yes, we received quite a revelation when we witnessed the dragon enter these regions again. They have been extinct for years now, and the first sight of one here made us stop and think that maybe something in these lands is preparing to rekindle the past. A terrifying prospect for us elementals as you would no doubt agree. Why, if man ever went back to the old ways…Imagine the devastation!'

'I am sure that isn't the case,' replied Marl with certainty.

'But it was real, I tell you.' The tree began to stress. 'Large as life! It flew close to the town, hurling flame from its maw. It journeyed in that direction.'

Treebon pointed towards the road and the mountains beyond.

'I did not believe it at first.'

'There is a dragon,' Marl concluded, 'but not a dragon. It is our firm belief that what you witnessed was nothing more than an imposter, a saboteur, a shapeshifter that can alter his appearance to look like a dragon.'

'You cannot be serious! No trickster is that powerful. No mage is that convincing. A man can look like a dragon, though cannot breathe fire that hot that it turns metal to ash in seconds. It is but a trick!'

'It is no trick, my friend. The Sinistrom have abilities and weapons unknown to many who merely wield magic. Their knowledge is far older than ours.'

'Well,' said Treebon, cautiously, 'if you are going to chase this creature I hope that you will heed my warning: if you find this dragon or trickster or whatever it is, please bear in mind that it is still a dragon, and dragons, the most nefarious of their kind, are also the most vicious and perilous. Please take care, my old friend. All of you! Take good care of yourselves!'

Marl, Treebon, and A-Sap shook hands a second time and went their separate ways. The mages made their lengthy trek along the straight road, while Treebon and A-Sap remained to clear away the death and destruction left behind by the town's recent occupants.

Marl explained to Fabian upon leaving that Treebon and A-Sap would stay behind to cleanse the ghost town of any remaining evil and then renew its former beauty. They would plant flowers in the gardens and sow trees in the graveyards. Steadily, but surely, people would come back to the town from distant places and colonise it.

'Soon that evil town will swell with the happy laughter of children.'

The prince looked sad as he stroked the long dark tresses of his steed.

'Does this bother you?' Marl asked.

Fabian regarded the town as he and the other mages made their way to the outskirts.

'That thing that attacked me…'

'That thing was nothing more than an evil aberration, a puppet. There are many dangers, I'll have you know, Master Fabian, and many of these creatures will not hesitate to use your sentimentality against you. We did the right thing here.'

'It doesn't feel right. I think of those poor people and feel remorse.'

'Those people have been dead now for a long time. Hopefully now they'll be able to rest peacefully and do so without evil's influence. Come, we have a long journey ahead of us.'

'Wait!' Fabian said, pointing to something that had obviously caught his attention. 'What is that?'

Marl followed the boy's gaze to a small object glinting in the sun.

'I see it. I don't know.'

Inquisitively, Fabian made his way to where he saw the shiny mass. It was partially concealed amidst tall grass in a thicket surrounded by green hedges. As the boy approached the object began to look more and more familiar. It was metallic and box shaped. Why, it was Tør's holographic cube emitter, the one he'd shown Fabian during his short stay in Mundor.

Curiously, Marl observed the boy bring the object back.

'What did you find?'

Fabian glanced down at the object in his hand.

'Something that belonged to the ambassador.'

Marl looked at the other mages, and then peered up at the sky.

'It would seem that our good ambassador came this way after all. It also corroborates Treebon's story. Come!' He instructed, pulling on the reins of his steed. 'We have a full day ahead of us and I wish to reach the mountains by nightfall!'

Fabian placed the device in his pocket and mounted his horse.

Chapter 10

The bridge officers watched as the small ship prepared to leave the docking port. It was seen on the view screen, the aft thrusters sending out quick, sharp jets of antimatter.

'Detach mooring clamps,' spoke the com technician.

'Mooring clamps are detached, sir.' Came the confirmation. 'Malecarjan's ship is clear of the docking port.'

Cougar Chuko gave a toothy smile as he stared up at the view screen. He thought of the prisoner in his hold, the ambassador, a VIP of a sort. What a world of opportunity he presented! Why, he thought with a devious flick of his tongue, he could hold the Sinistrom ambassador to ransom. He could make money, more money than the gods themselves. Or perhaps he could make even more money if he just allowed the ambassador to simply die—to die horribly in front of a paying crowd of people! Now this idea had possibilities!

'That pompous ass,' Cougar said under his breath as he watched Malecarjan's shuttle speed off into the great blue yonder. 'I'll be damned if I'm keeping such an important prisoner around in my dungeons. That is inviting trouble. I have other plans for our…guest. You see, I love to play these games dangerously. I suppose I am a sadistic brute at heart. But I love the challenge. This is what'll give me an all time high, because I know with the proper leverage there isn't a damn thing any of my victims can do to stop me. And I receive a higher turnover. Merely an added bonus. So this is what I am going to do: first I am going to torture our "guest" to amuse a mob. I will make Tør fight for his very existence in the arena. Malecarjan said, "no disintegrations. But I will have that grim-looking swine so dependant and wrapped around my finger, he won't be in any condition to object.'

Cougar Chuko pressed a button that activated a small video feed. The screen came to life and transmitted an image. A view of a large room in the lower levels of Urban Cloud presented itself to his gaze. This room was only slightly lit, with straw and what appeared to be gnawed bones littering the floor. Horrific, loud groans indicated that the room was indeed occupied by something large, a beast of some description.

'I believe it is time we put on a little show for our… guest,' he muttered with a grin.

The ambassador sat in his cell, chained to the wall. *These guest quarters are far from adequate*, he thought to himself miserably as the guard stood outside, ever primed and ready for the slightest movement or possible insurgency—as if the force field obstructing the entrance to his cell wasn't enough.

Tør looked up at the pig-faced guard. He wondered if such a creature could be bribed in any way. These Head Hunters were always after gold or money, and the ambassador's father had plenty to offer.

Alternately, he could stage a diversion and get the guard to be distracted for a moment while he stole the guy's keys. Ah, what was he thinking? The pig-faced moron wouldn't even be distracted by his own foul odour.

The ambassador sat back, folding his arms glumly. No, there was no use at all! He would just have to sit tight until some kind of ransom was paid. No doubt his father would come through for him before long.

In his mind, suddenly, he could hear the sounds of voices calling out in pain, and then fading into silence. Tør looked around, thinking that it had come from an adjacent cell. But it was far too sharp, too accurate for that. No, it was more of a thought, a memory, and far too local to have come from anything in the immediate vicinity. Could it have been telepathy maybe? He could not say. It came again, louder than before. He had to clasp his hands flat against his ears this time, though the sounds were indeed in his head and could not so easily be shut out. He caught a brief picture in his mind, a vague image of an orb glowing brightly and brilliantly in a room no larger than the cell he inhabited. The orb in his mind cried out in rage. The guard remained ignorant of the noise which apparently only the prisoner could hear.

Beyond the glow of the orb were several winged reptiles. Tør recognised them as dragons. He could remember reading about them in the books and fairy tales of his home world. These dragons were bright gold, though their affluent tincture had at once become dulled by the greed of their captors. He saw them imprisoned much like he was, and they were calling for help. They were calling to him. Descriptive imagery cascaded into his mind, a story of a life being told via telepathic link. These dragons were demonstrating that they were being used by their cruel masters, the Head Hunters, to gain profit and wealth. Their powers were diminishing as more people came to steal it from them. Tør swallowed as the sheer cruelty of the matter hit him full on in his mind's eye. These creatures were nothing more than batteries to the Head Hunters. They were being used as transformers of a sort, and were being made to relinquish portions of their great powers to enhance and energise those who had come seeking such power. This power would be transplanted and stolen from its original owners and offered to anyone with deep enough pockets to pay for it.

Tør did not know how to respond to this plea for help, but somehow he could sense their pain. These dragons were getting weaker.

'How can I help you?' the prisoner cried out.

Hearing this sudden outburst, the guard turned to face the ambassador.

'Quiet!' He grunted. 'What is up with you? Are you ill?'

Tør clutched his head between his hands, his forehead furrowed, and his mouth twisted with the discomfort of the onward barrage. Images pressed against his mind, dark and painful to behold, and the sounds were getting more and more voluble and unbearable.

Suddenly, the voices stopped. With his heart still knocking on his ribs, Tør looked up with a certain relief, though could still feel the emotion left behind by those who had just tried to communicate with him.

Dragons, he thought. *Are these the same dragons that kidnapped me?* Until that moment in the market, when the danger came so swiftly, he had thought these creatures were nothing more than the figments of myth and the imagination. It took a real fire breathing dragon to teach him that not all myths were fabrications.

Several hours had passed since the mages left that god forsaken town. The sun had begun to dip behind the mountains toward the west, taking with it the scorching heat, as well as the uneasy humidity and threat of dehydration.

They reached a rocky valley surrounded by cacti and a smattering of gum trees. Dry in appearance, the spinifex grass grew in clumps amid stark rock formations, some of which rose like lofty plateaux harbouring accesses to underground caves, grottos that went on for miles beneath the sun scorched earth.

'We'll set up camp over there.' Marl suggested, pointing over at one of the plateaux several meters away.

From a neighbouring plateau, a pair of eyes watched with apparent interest as the new arrivals set up camp. Tweak felt that maybe this little spying venture he had embarked upon was going to take forever. But this venture had excited his curiosity more and more.

As night fell the temperature dropped considerably. A fire began to blaze as the seven mages sat telling stories of their endeavours. As it turned out, all of the mages were ex-military, veterans of a sort. Prince Fabian was eager to hear their various narratives. As it happened, Justas Marl started his career as a centurion at Aspiren, a city thousands of miles north of Mundor. He went on to explain that he left that vocation after only three months and went on to become a barrister, like his father before him.

'From soldier to notary…in just three months?' Questioned Fabian, looking surprised. 'That is quite a leap!'

'Ah, but I was never happy as an infantry soldier.' The man explained. 'I was more interested in law and justice than I was defending the corrupt laws of the state. I was like most, blinded by career, but truth is, I didn't really have the heart for it. I was doing what was expected of me: I made money and lived in a modest dwelling alone. Until the day I realised the truth: money, duty, and security are poor substitutes for immortality.'

'Immortality?' enquired the prince, looking askance. 'You mean like living forever sort of thing?'

'I am talking about immortality in the numinous sense.' Explained the other. 'That instance when you shift from one set of beliefs to come wholly upon a fresh state of mind, which we call an epiphany, is the state of being that becomes connected with everything around you. But when you stumble upon a new awareness you discover that all the old worldly trappings no longer hold any power over your thinking. The old world falls away like a shadow passing over a lake. The old me, that is the mortal me, would not have left home to travel. I lived from day to day afraid of taking a leap without safety nets. I paid my taxes. I grew frustrated. I drank a lot to forget my irritation, my indisposition. Death had me in its maw. Not death as in finality, I speak of the death in life: the death of inaction, the death of being always trapped in the same rut. Finally, death shall teach us the simple truth. We can only drag ourselves up from the mire. But man's work always takes priority over life. What is achieved by all this mundane activity, then? I desire life without measure. But I attained it by taking root and thinking about the problem, the eternal problem. In the early days I had my father's law books to inspire me. I wanted truth. I realised that I did not need the law as my ally. If a politician wants anything it is always self serving, not for the good of the people.

If a law maker wants anything, it is truth. True he has the law to back him up, and the law can be a difficult taskmaster it is true, and sometimes the law can deny us the justice the heart oft desires, but I believed that one man could make the difference. I believed that if there was any wisdom and beauty in the world, the law could make it safe and preserve the ideals as well as the people that were most dear to me. I suppose I was young and naïve. In the end, politics always intrudes. Greed is the mother of all kings, and the law is her servant. I trusted too easily in those days and was slow to question.

'Now take a look at me. I have lived out my mortality and have pulled myself back from death. I am in tune to everything now. Even the stones, that lay strewn along the dusty earth, bear a resonance. I am attuned to the vibrations of the soil. Each and every one of us has a story. Each mage has a unique tale to tell, an anecdote born of not so unique beginnings.'

'So, let's hear your stories.' The young prince felt impelled to ask the others.

Colonel Warclaw smiled and instantly he sprang straight into the spirit of things by giving his account.

'I've always been a soldier. Though I haven't always looked like this.'

He gestured at his own face, knowing how unusual

it looked. His skin was a deep blue with scales, and his eyes could actually extend outwards on stalks, much like that of a shrimp or crustacean. He had plenty of armour covering both his shins and his torso, though most of this was part of what he called his exoskeleton.

'I was part of a platoon that was sent to the Coast of Kurln. If you have ever been to the Coast of Kurln you would know that those golden beaches boast the greatest treasures known to man, as well as the most pernicious curses and traps ever devised by ancient man. Well, our king, a man known as Solomon, ordered ten of us to fetch the riches of which had been spoken in legend. Truly, we were dubious about making such a perilous trek into such unknown territories, especially once we had heard the tales, the terrifying fictions based upon those coastlines. Sometimes even fictions have a flicker of truth to them. But the king's word was law, so we made the long trek. Once we arrived we discovered the treasures of which had been burned in legend. We filled our sacks with gold, pearls, and as many trinkets as we could carry. Only two of us made it off that coast that day. The other eight in our platoon were either buried, or eaten, or were simply taken without any warning, never to be heard from again. I and my second in command, Iron May, were the only two survivors, if that is what you can call us. The curse came upon us when we tried to steal the gems. I don't quite know what took place, it all happened so quickly. Iron May here was transformed into something completely other worldly, while I became this…this thing you see today. May's flesh turned to metal. I watched in dismay as these spikes, as hard steel, emerged from her arms and legs like daggers! We became these things for only a brief time, and then we returned to normal. We were afraid, though gathering from what we could read from the old cave scriptures there was a penance. The scriptures were written in stone, most of which was difficult to read due to time and erosion, but from what we could gather the penance involved a transformation, a modification of both strength and physical appearance. We had become these things of great strength and power, though provisionally. The scriptures said that we had been ordained to guard the treasure for the rest of our natural lives and that if we ever tried to leave that place we would go back to looking like freaks of nature: May with her metal skin and, of course, me with my odd appearance.

'True, we could not stay for very long. Our situation unfortunately was forced upon us by our king. This time it was Solomon who came in person and he was accompanied by his seventh legion. He and his men had travelled the long distance to the coast to find out what had happened to us. He was angry and thought that we had abandoned him, deciding after all to take his treasure for our own. Of course, we had been mutated to guard the treasure at all costs. The curse of the grotto forced us once again to become these aberrations. The curse gave us weapons and a prowess with hand to hand combat, as well as great magic abilities to repel our former king and his army. Being the total cowards that we were we did not disagree with our new and terrifying mistress—this age old curse that forced us to fight. We went out onto the beach and we slaughtered every last one of our former kinsmen. King Solomon, obviously, had no idea that it was us. Not that it mattered much since it was Iron May here who sliced off his head.'

'And I would do it again.' She spoke honestly and with much venom in her words. 'Like Marl said, if it wasn't for the politics and the self-serving greed of kings I would still be human.'

'We stayed at the grotto for a time,' Warclaw continued, 'and remained human for as long as we endured there, but a prison is a prison still, even if that prison promises normality. We headed away from the coast, and the further we travelled away from the origin of our curse the more we began to resemble said curse. We are freaks, true, but we found companionship within the brotherhood of mages. We learned to master our anger and channel it for good, though the memory of slaughter and the recollection of a king that betrayed us remains a constant reminder to us both that life is full of treachery. But we also learned that friendship and honour are something earned, not simply offered to others as though it were their birthright.'

'That is an impressive anecdote to be sure,' remarked Centorionn with a mild mannered tone. 'My story is perhaps a little less impressive to be honest.'

'Tell us.' Prompted Fabian with interest. 'How did you become half horse, half man?'

'Oh, I was born this way. All of my people are segregated like this. We lived to the south, far beyond the great ocean of turbulence. There aren't that many of us left. Those of us that remain are a simple, though peaceful, people. We never made any trouble for anyone else, well, not until the ogres and giants came with their great appetites and their hunger for industry. They turned us into beasts of burden, and those of us who could not work they turned into livestock and ate us. I was one of the few lucky ones who survived their tyranny.'

Fabian considered Centorionn's story with confusion.

'But I thought that the Ogres and giants were allies of the Sinistrom,' said the young man, his brow furrowed.

'Yes,' Centorionn answered. 'They were allied eventually. And the Sinistrom did bring peace and concordance to our respective peoples. They fed the giants. And brought both sides into their fold. But that was many years after all the atrocities had been committed.'

'Did you have a family, friends, back in the south beyond the sea?' asked the prince, feeling saddened by Centorionn's account.

The segregated creature just nodded, allowing a tear to trickle down his left cheek.

'I had a life. If ever there was a time I felt truly at peace it was with my family, and wife, and children…All of whom I have not seen in a very long time.'

Centorionn fiddled with his bow string as he endeavoured to keep his emotions under check.

There was a sombre silence for a moment. Then Fabian asked the question:

'Will you ever see them again?'

There was a moment or two's hesitation as the mage wiped his face with the back of his wrist. The wounds had not been healed completely by time, and the creature was far too tired and weary to fight his sorrow that welled within him.

'Excuse me,' he said, and rose to his feet (all four of them). As he walked away, Fabian got up and sprinted over to him. Such a dear and gentle creature he was, and Fabian felt so terribly awful about dredging up the past as he evidently had.

'I'm sorry,' he said as Centorionn stopped dead in his tracks.

'About what...?'

'I should not have asked about your people.'

Centorionn smiled and patted the boy gently on the back.

'No, I am a silly old fool. It has been years now and I should not be so thin skinned about it all.'

'You still miss them, don't you?'

The creature looked down at the ground forlornly.

'I can barely hide it. Sometimes I look at my reflection and see myself as others must see me: as a beast filled with violence. My face, rudely cast, is a brute's face.'

'I don't see that at all,' said the prince, reaching out with a gentle hand. 'I see a gentle man, a sincere, tender man.'

'That used to be true...before the dark days. Truth is, I seek revenge. I have sought retribution since it all started, since I watched those I love become food for the terrible creatures that preyed on us. I killed those townsfolk today, not out of self defence, but rather out of retribution. Every time I go into battle I see the faces of those who did me harm all those years ago.'

'They weren't human. They weren't even alive in the purest sense.'

'That may be true, but that does not excuse how I felt,' the creature said, putting his hands before his eyes in shame. 'The truth remains, those people were human once, had lives and had people who cared for them. I am no different, or indeed no better than the ogres and giants who still terrorise my dreams. I live out my passion and people get hurt.'

'That is not true. And you are being too hard on yourself. You know it.'

The two were eventually joined by Katt Brutal and Marl. Both were deeply concerned for their four-legged companion.

'It's alright,' said Fabian, 'he's fine. He's just a little tired.'

'Okay,' replied Marl, nodding his head. 'It has been a long journey. You should rest my friend. We have a long day ahead of us tomorrow.'

'I know,' Centorionn said, turning away. The night hid the tears in his eyes.

'You'll be okay?' asked Katt.

'I'll stay with him,' answered Fabian, taking hold of Centorionn's arm.

As the two entered the tent, Centorionn began to lie down on the ground. A satin pillow cradled his head. Fabian knelt down behind the creature's back and gently he placed his hand flat against his hair, caressing his thick mane of brown locks.

'Thank you,' the creature said, deeply appreciating the affection.

'Hush. Go to sleep.'

The young man continued to stroke the long thick hair as though caressing a cat.

Fabian waited till Centorionn was fast asleep before steadily and quietly deciding to leave and rejoin the others.

'He's sleeping peacefully,' he told them as he perched himself by the fire.

'You have a parental nature.' Marl observed with a smile. 'I like that.'

'I guess I had my mother to thank for that.' Fabian responded, realising what a major part she played in his development. 'She taught me how to take care of myself.

My father was always too busy with stately matters to care one way or another what happened to me.'

The chief mage nodded and said:

'Though most boys in my experience who have feminine natures – and I hope you don't think me rude in saying this – have more than just a mother's influence. Usually the motivations lie behind the fact of growing up in a large family, with lots of sisters. Sometimes the male, if older than his siblings, feels obliged to act more masculine in order to provide and protect said siblings, while a brother, perhaps much younger than his sisters, would feel more obligated to fit in as it were, to appreciate more feminine attributes.'

'I am an only child,' answered the prince honestly. 'I never had any sisters or brothers.'

'Then conceivably there is some other influence at work here. Your alter ego is an influence perhaps. I don't know. I am only guessing. The Dragon Tolan which you become may be female, or indeed feminine enough to have its very nature rub off on you while you are still in human form. Who's to say? None-the-less, I find this concept new and fascinating.'

Katt Brutal perched herself on a stone next to Fabian and, placing a clawed hand on the boy's shoulder, said:

'Whatever the reason, we girls should stick together!'

Fabian laughed heartily in response to this.

'So, Kat, what about you? What's your story?'

The cat-like entity thought about her life for a second. Truthfully, the cat was pampered as all cats were invariably. She smiled a wide, energetic smile and leapt into the telling of her story.

'I was from the same province as Centorionn. We were pets to the ogres. They built us litter trays, and they groomed us and fed us.'

'Fed you what?' Fabian said, shooting Kat a sudden look of astonishment.

'Meat, of course, what else do owners feed their cats?'

Fabian looked flabbergasted.

'Does Centorionn know about this?!'

'What do I look like—bloody oracle?' Katt replied temperamentally and leapt from the stone she had been perched upon.

Fabian blinked, unable to register her apparent lack of shame.

It was then Dreathor's turn to tell them a story. He started in that hearty, though loud, croaky voice the others had come to know and love: 'I was neither cursed or blessed. I simply am, in a manner of speaking. And what I am, in basic terms, is a man carved quite literally from stone. I guess the sculptor who created me was either very blind or had no talent in the art of crafting beauty from igneous rock. But man, he must have known how to breathe life into his creations, clearly, or else I wouldn't be here now, telling this story to you. But that was a long, long time ago. I don't even recall what the old geezer looked like. But I do recall other thing. For example, I remember the last time I was out here. I came across a trio of mountain trolls. Bear in mind, it was a Monday if memory serves. Bad things tend to happen on a Monday in any case. Though I do not know why people hate that particular day so much. It is a day just like any other. I believe the reason is so noted in the collective conscience because it is the first day that marks our defeat. But I digress. Now, where was I? Where was I going with this? Now I've completely lost my train of thought!'

'Trolls.' Prompted the young prince.

'Ah, yes, trolls! That's right! None of whom were very intelligent and neither were they particularly pretty, but they had stolen a bunch of clothes and dresses from a passing caravan of unlucky traders and proceeded to put them on. Now trolls aren't particularly dainty creatures as you have no doubt been told, and neither were the women they stole the clothes from to be totally honest, but these three ugly morons were trying on these dresses, thinking that they looked all splendid and dainty. Well, I of course, being of sound mind and, incidentally, sound gender, decided to approach these indigent morons and, with all the dignity I could muster, asked them which way to the bathroom. Now, this particular line of enquiry, as you probably know, is most offensive to a troll since during the times of the vile unrest there was a certain troll king who once resided over these here valleys. Casting my mind back to the legend of King Dunny, 'ere was a potentate, a fat old troll who sat upon a gold throne. But one day his throne wouldn't flush properly and he called his fellow subjects and trolls to council. Well, there was one particularly stupid troll going by the name of Burk who actually thought he was a dab hand at plumbing. As it turned out, the poor old king trusted Burk to fix the problem, and when he was asked to test his throne out after he'd scoffed down a curry and fries he was then swallowed into the pipework and was never seen again. Of course, this sad case of affairs has always been a bit of a sore spot with trolls in general and they found my question to be insulting to say the least. Well, the three jeepers creepers first looked at me, then at each other, as you do, and said in a tone louder than a fog horn "bee bi bo bum…who the hell do you think you are, buster?" Well,

I flatly told them that particular query didn't rhyme, and that all trolls speak in a corresponding syntax of terminal sounds of words or of lines of verse. Well, the big sissy blew a damn hissy fit, didn't he? And told me where I could go stick it. Well, I told the dickens that if he didn't start talking polite an' all, I'd be obliged to find the washroom all on me lonesome. He said fine and I tore the fella's dress. He wasn't too impressed with that, I can tells yah. His friends looked pretty mean, but I was meaner. I looked at the one with the wonky eye and I said, "hey, Lilly, how did you get to be so flamin' ugly!" and he ran off crying. I couldn't believe it. He actually picked up his damn ball gown and fled into the desert crying his bleedin' eyes out. Great hairy twit! The other troll decided to come at me with a club, so me, who just happened to be wearing a regimental skirt and very little in the way of underwear, decided to reveal all. The big brute fell down in a big shaggy heap on the floor. "Now" I said to the one who was left standin', grabbing him by the dewlaps, "which way to the toilet?"'

The others just stared blankly at Draethor, wondering if maybe this charming little tale was going to lead anywhere, but knowing Draethor it probably wasn't. There was a protracted silence before Katt Brutal laughed and remarked,

'You know, your stories really crack me up…dewlaps!' And she chortled even louder.

'Okay,' said Iron May, grabbing Katt's plate, 'I think you've had quite enough lizard curry for one evening.'

'You really do need to understand the subtleties of troll mores and morays to appreciate the joke.' Draethor endeavoured to justify his little anecdote. 'If not, then throw in a word like "dewlaps" and it becomes funny none-the-less.' The man of stone added, shrugging his shoulders.

'So then,' the prince quickly changed the subject, 'how did you all become mages?'

Justas Marl took a sip of his soup and then answered:

'Well, how did you become a mage? Our story, I would guess, is no different than yours.'

The prince stared at the older man blankly.

'Magical powers were thrust on us whether we wanted it or not.' Continued Marl, blankly. 'We each have powers of our own, unique to each and every one of us.'

Marl closed his eyes. The expression on his face was one of serenity as the bird tattoo repositioned itself, moving to the centre of his face and then shifted to the opposite side. It was fully animate. It was only an ink outline, though it had taken on a life of its own.

'How do you control your tattoo like that?' asked the young man.

'Easy. It just takes a little bit of focus.'

'You try. Focus on your ability.' Commanded the man of stone. 'Call upon the Dragon Tolan. That is your power.'

Prince Fabian was unsure. His dragon persona had always revealed itself in certain situations when trouble seemed to brew. He had never called on the power before.

After a goading from his fellow mages he stood up, walked to a safe distance and began to try, first closing his eyes, tightening his lids as though there was a great fiery sun in the sky and it was blinding him.

Justas Marl rose to his feet.

'It is alright, my young friend,' he said. 'In time you will learn the trick of transformation. Great physical change is hard to muster. For me, the act is a simple manipulation of ink in the skin to move from one place to another in formation. For you, the art of conversion must take more mental concentration. You'll get the hang of it.'

The prince relaxed himself. He then began to cast his mind back to his mother. The tenderness of feeling merged with the sensation of prominent danger, integrating thought into corporeal awareness—the image of her broken body in the snow, and the howl of those wolves still fresh in his thoughts.

'I- I can't do it!' he stammered, opening his eyes.

'You will, in time,' Marl told him.

'What if I never learn?' the prince replied, despondently. 'What if I cannot save Mundor? Or make my father understand that I have these feelings and abilities?'

Something in Fabian's words made Marl think that maybe some other emotion, some fear was impeding this boy from reaching his full potential. He nodded suddenly and said:

'An artist, much like a mage, has an uncanny ability to make use of his talents simply by seeing. That which can be seen by the eye can just as easily be destroyed by the eye as well. Sight is the father of all accomplishments, as it is the mother of annihilation. You must first master annihilation and death before you can muster the transformation you seek.'

'I don't understand. You say I have to die before I can master this thing?' the prince asked, confused.

'I did not mean to use the word death so literally.' Came the glib reply. 'Death is simply a beginning. It is like the complex caterpillar that changes into a beautiful butterfly. Death comes about as you realise that what you have learnt is a lie, and begin to live your life as destiny sees fit. Defeat and death are not bad things, and they are definitely nothing to be feared. Though, many people fear change. Both life and defeat are inseparable as one leads invariably to the other. The man whom the elect calls artist or magician knows this. He knows too that his fellow man is putrescent with fear and trepidation. Alone, the artist has courage…the courage to see.

'I trust in my own destiny. I have walked my own destiny, made my own rules, and have lived my own life and am happy. How many people in your not-so-broad experience can say the same? Be under no illusion, this is not arrogance speaking, it is merely certainty. Man's greatest defeat came during the great cataclysm. Our history books tell of the day when magic stole technology. Though, it wasn't enough of a defeat to lead mankind to the next phase of awareness. He still hides behind a comfortable lie. But one day, perhaps, he will see the road to destiny in more lateral terms than he does now. Because, in that moment, he will hit rock bottom and find only the truth. The truth that life, much like art, is not linear as he first imagined, but indeed disordered, tangential, spreading outwards, and downwards, and inwards, like a tree bearing fruit. That which the cultivated man has denied himself for centuries will one day fall apart. It is inevitable. But you must be brave, my young friend. You must dare to look deep into the chasm and overcome everything you know, every fibre and falsehood which you have learned. You must take a blind leap in the mysterious realms of the unknown world and measure the deep, and then turn your gaze inward to the knowledge, the understanding that retains its certitude in the natural world. With sight you will come to see your ending, objective, and your heart's impasse. You will see your present, your past, and future before your very eyes, and the ability to drop everything. To recreate yourself in order to be transformed. And it is a transformation you seek. A revolution of mind, body and spirit as all of these attributes are asynchronous, and central in the creation of what you must achieve.'

'You speak in riddles!' the boy said, folding his arms dejectedly.

'I speak an old language…ancient in fact, and yet it is a language not yet conceived. It is not a riddle, but the natural truth. Ask yourself, how would you be able to move beyond the known, beyond the safety net of home without even a scrap of courage? The only real problem you face at present, Fabian, is that the life you have known is constantly holding you back. I would be inclined to call it tunnel vision, a sight so narrow it hinders the very transformation you seek. True, you have the desire to see, but desire is but the flame overshadowed by fear. By your own admissions I am able to deduce that you wish to win favour with your father and redeem yourself in his eyes. You even said that you wished to save Mundor. But what if I told you that you had nothing to prove?'

The prince looked at once puzzled.

'What do you mean? I know I have nothing to prove.'

'My boy, your thoughts appear to be arrested by a notion.'

'What notion?' asked Fabian.

'The notion that your life is ransomed by the very people you claim to serve. And you would be correct in that belief. Fabian, my bright, shining boy, you have a gift. You have an amazing ability. And yet it has been overlooked. I am guessing that is no longer the case though, since I think, maybe, some of your people have grown aware of your transformation. And I think that is what forced you to venture out this far. The truth is they fear you. They misunderstand you. So not only does your gift go unnoticed for a time, now they persecute and single you out. In fact, they've pushed you out. Instead of instructing you, they cast you from their bosom.'

Awkwardly, Fabian looked away.

'I know it isn't fair.' Marl continued. 'It isn't right. Especially since you have a lot to learn. It was a great philosopher who once said: "The structures of man are but a stitch in time. They also fester, forging a way for emotional as well as physical enslavement." What we call education is anything but. Not when systems of instruction overlook the individual talent of a single boy or girl. Our towns and cities, our schools, and religious icons, for the present moment, are structures that continue to penetrate and pervade. Children are products of fear. Institutions must churn out product on a yearly basis. I would indeed refer to civilised children as product, as that is exactly how they have been treated. They are sent out into the world, motivated to err the same as their parents, and their parents before them. Nothing changes. The wheels keep on turning. Who cares about making magic and having sight or courage when instruction tells us to trust in the realist? When instruction tells us that we cannot move mountains or part oceans in an attempt to live our lives as we should? Kings, law makers, and merchants are all alike, all schemers. Particularly in the skill of creating mandates whereby all parties have to adhere to a certain comedy of routine. They would murder original thought. They have all but massacred instinct. I know these things because I have lived apart from society. I have turned a critical eye to the world and recognise its double standards. I also know that the mage, much like the artist follows his own star, his own rules; therefore he is lifted to the higher level, not because he knows how to follow, no, because he knows primarily how to lead.'

'I don't get it,' said the young man, frustrated. 'You say that men must learn to walk their own paths, but how can this be allowed if such men turn to structures of leadership? Men cannot be themselves if they are permitted to follow. I find your argument inconsistent.'

Marl made a sound of laughter.

'My boy, you take everything literally.'

The young man narrowed his eyes.

'Here. Look,' said the older mage. 'Let me tell you a little secret. I don't care if you learn from me or not. I don't care that you follow me. I would rather that you didn't. What I do care about is that you care. Yes?'

The young man nodded tentatively.

'You care,' Marl said. 'You have come this far. Now I can only lead by example. I was once where you are today. Part and prey to a system that would not recognise my gifts even if it pulled its collected head out of the sphincter of its own making. Right now, you could use guidance. Everyone needs guidance. That is where true equality lies, in the understanding between teacher and pupil. There has to be an equal footing, otherwise the pupil can learn nothing.'

'But not all men are truly equal,' answered the boy. 'The king is not equal to the man who tends the stable, or the washer woman who scours the linen.'

'Well, I think that we have now touched on a truth, albeit a very unfortunate one. And do you believe yourself to be equal to your so-called peers, Fabian? Do you believe that a boy of 10 years is equal to his teachers, his father, mother, when he sits in class, unable to understand or grasp what these paid monkeys are saying, when they are explaining the square root of shapes, or defending the wills of capricious gods in their religious classes? When a child falls behind on his or her studies simply because they are not suited to the schoolwork that is set for them? Is a person equal then? Are they all on the same emotional and intellectual page? What do you imagine your king and farther would say if he were to learn of your feelings for the ambassador? Do you believe that he would see eye to eye with you, and agree that a man can indeed lay down with another man?

You know straight away what his answer would be. So where is this equality which these religious institutions preach? It is a fallacy. That's the double standard! See, my point is this: the man who would be a mage or artist is nothing to society and its rules of conduct. The artist does not belong.'

'But we have artists as we have wizards. They belong. We don't treat them any differently from, lets say, the man who makes horseshoes.' Fabian made the sudden argument. 'We have a court magician. He entertains the royal house with tricks and distracts us with artifice. And our artists create tapestries depicting battles. They make portraits of great people. They paint religious icons and—'

'That is not art, my boy, it is merely technique. And preferred systems of practice will always be more widely accepted than art per se.' The man continued to educate. 'There we go again, misunderstanding popular definitions and giving them literal meaning. But I will tell you the true definition of things. The distinction between mage and magician is sight. It is awareness. Awareness comes from within. Whereas a magician does as he is told, a mage listens to the voice that comes from within. That voice is within you, Fabian. It comes from that unique place. And that awareness will transform you, believe me. You will transform because you have partial sight already. And you are brave. One day...One day you may open your eyes and become the leader you were born to be. You will lead by example. You will be the new principal of change for your people. I see that this idea frightens you. As you misinterpret the difference between art and technique, you also mistake the distinction between leadership and rule. Most fools can rule men. A true leader can influence by example. He can influence another man to do great things. He may not change society by and large, but he can take a lost soul and guard it against the lie. This is what I am doing with you. I am trying to help you to open your eyes. I can only open the door for you. You have ability within you to walk through it. I see this ability. Few other people do, which is clear. And it takes great courage to stand alone against the grain, and in the face of truth. But you have to come upon this realisation by yourself. No one can do it for you. No one else is going to transform your life. Only you can open your eyes, Fabian. Only you can change.'

The boy was silent trying to take it all in.

'In the end, it is sight and only sight that will give you the power of will necessary to accomplish great things.'

Maybe the boy would take it on board and discover

that sight was attained by the simple reflex of opening one's eyes. In the end, there was really nothing to it.

The camp fire had been reduced to embers by the time the six mages had fallen asleep. All but one: Marl had agreed to remain awake. Close by, Tweak positioned himself behind a pinnacle of stone. Quietly opening one of the pouches he kept suspended about his belt he inhaled its powdery contents. It glittered and sparkled magically as it entered his nose, transforming the strange looking dwarf into a form of fowl: a duck. He then waddled around the pinnacle. Marl sang softly to himself as he watched the diminishing flame. And, silently, the tiny patter of webbed feet went completely unnoticed.

Tweak made his way past the encampment. A short distance away stood the mouth to a deep cave. *That must be where the ambassador is being kept,* Tweak reasoned as he regarded the cruel Fabian and his vile friends. Yes, the ambassador had to be here, or else why would these mages be guarding this cave if not to keep this poor prisoner captive?

Tweak made his ascent to the mouth of the cave. He heard Fabian groan in his sleep behind him and stopped dead, believing the despicable creature had awoken suddenly. The duck turned to look behind. Fabian had merely turned over in his slumber and continued to be unaware. Marl was humming a poignant tune. Exhaling a sigh of relief, the duck continued up the steep hillside. His tiny webbed feet navigated the stony ground. Then he did something he could not explain. He made a sound. A loud quack resonated down the hill and into the valley where Marl stopped singing abruptly. The mage looked up from the fire. That was not a sound typical to these parts. Tweak hastened his step, flapping his wings frantically. *Damn this magic*, he thought. *Why did I have to quack?* The sound had come involuntarily. It was just a needless and adverse affect of using magic. Because of one reckless quack the mage noticed the animal, though it was too dark to see what it was. His attentions soon returned to the burning embers before him. The fire was almost out. More wood was required. As Marl lent over to reach for fresh fuel he failed to notice the duck as it settled behind him. The shape altered. The duck's shadowy profile grew in size and stature along the ground, betraying Tweak's true form. The startled man turned round. Tweak wafted the magical contents of his pouch in Marl's face.

'Sleep.' The dwarf commanded.

The mage fell unconscious over a stack of firewood.

Tweak took this opportunity to attempt to traverse the hill a second time. The mouth of the cave lay beyond. This time Tweak lost his footing, slipped and caused several stones to go tumbling.

Fabian woke with a start and went for his sword. Tweak charged up the hill the rest of the way and managed to reach the mouth of the cave to avoid further detection.

The stones came to a halt by the embers as Fabian rose to investigate. The other mages were still asleep. Someone else was here. There were footprints in the dry earth which did not belong to either he or his friends.

Extracting his sword, Fabian began to climb the hillside. Tweak pressed his face against the rock and could plainly see the prince's silhouette emerging closer with each step. Quickly, the dwarf took retreat into the cave's inner sanctum. He could hear the sound of cascading water in the distance. Maybe it was an underground river or lagoon. Maybe he could lose the prince there somehow, he knew how tenacious Fabian could be.

Looking behind, Tweak caught a glimpse of the boy's outline against the moon as he approached the entrance.

'Show yourself, whoever you are! I know you're in here!'

Tweak began to panic. He hid in the darkness of the cave, afraid of the blackness that encapsulated him, though even more afraid of the consequences should he be found. He took his chances with the darkness. Following the sound of water, Tweak made his way deeper into the cave.

There was some light leaking in from a shallow tunnel high above. This offered some peace of mind at least. A short distance away the angry shouts of 'Coward, show yourself!' continued as the prince searched.

Tweak entered a grotto, the home of an underground river at the foot of a huge, cascading waterfall. He found a niche in the cave wall and hid himself within its murky confines.

He watched as the prince entered, letting his eyes examine the length and breadth of this yawning underground oasis. He also watched as the reckless youth entered the lake and began to wade outwards towards the falls. What was he doing? It was strange. It was like watching the involuntary amblings of a sleepwalker. Tweak rose steadily from his hiding place to get a better look. Most odd, he thought, watching as Fabian reached out with the tips of his fingers to touch the majestic waterfall.

It was at that precise moment Tweak remembered

the old fable from a book he had read. He went pale suddenly. Fear got the better of him. He jumped out of hiding, shouting a warning to the prince, but it was far too late. Fabian pressed his hands against the cascading waters. Just as the book had described, Fabian was pulled in. On the opposite side of the falls there was no oxygen, only water: dense, overpowering water. From that side of the cascade Fabian could not escape. The water was like thick glass. Desperately, the prince pounded his fists against the force of the torrent, but it was a wall, impenetrable. He was locked behind it, unable to breathe, incapable of calling for help.

Tweak didn't know what to do. Fabian was a villain, but even he did not deserve this kind of fate. Outside slept the other mages. Tweak had to warn them. He rushed out of the grotto and made his way towards the light of the moon. He knew every second he wasted would most likely be Fabian's last. He made such a racket as he lost his footing again, this time cartwheeling down the rocky ledge and waking several of the other mages. Stopping but a hair's breadth away from the still burning embers, and thanking his lucky stars that he had not caught fire as a result, Tweak opened his eyes at last to see five individuals standing over him.

'Hi.' He spoke a little clumsily and with a sense of embarrassment. Quickly, he came to his senses.

'Who are you?' Marl asked.

Draethor glanced down at the empty bed where Fabian had laid, then looked at the other mages.

'Where's Fabian?' he asked suddenly.

'Come quickly!' Tweak said. 'We haven't a moment to lose! Fabian is in trouble!'

'Quick, show us!' demanded Marl urgently.

Tweak led the mages into the cave, directing them to the grotto and the waterfall where the young prince had his hands flat against the impermeable wall of solid water. This was dark magic. The unfortunate boy was trapped behind the falls. He had been trying to force his way out to no avail. His lungs were about to give up.

'Don't touch the water!' Tweak warned. 'The water will pull you in just as it did Fabian!'

'Then how do we...?'

Tweak quickly noticed Draethor standing next to the waterfall.

'You idiot!' he shouted at the man of stone. 'You want to get sucked in as well?'

Draethor looked at the dwarf and snarled.

'Wait,' Marl said. 'The water is touching Draethor's arm.'

The dwarf cringed, fearful that the waters would claim another victim.

It didn't. The stone man appeared to be completely unaffected.

'Draethor,' said Marl. 'The water is touching you. The enchantment of the water must only recognise you as stone, not flesh. Quick. Grab Fabian.'

Slowly, Draethor placed his stony hand into the cascade. Moments later it emerged again holding the sagging frame of the water's recent victim.

'Place him down over there,' ordered Marl. Tweak helped Draethor to carry out the instruction. They waded through the waters until they reached the stony banks, and then placed the inanimate body down on the floor.

'Just hope I remember how to do this,' Marl muttered, bending over Fabian, pressing both his hands down over the boy's chest. He attempted to press down hard on the victim's chest. He removed his hands to administer oxygen by blowing into the Fabian's mouth. He repeated this over and over again, though there was no response. He pressed down again, counting the seconds as he did this, then shouting, 'Come on, damn you. Come on!' He forced his breath down the victim's throat, then again, and again. He then felt the gentle hand on his shoulder and the grim missive that their new friend was indeed dead.

Marl rose slowly, barely believing the evidence of his eyes.

'Fabian,' he said, leaning against the stone wall of the grotto for support. 'I would have followed him to the gates of the underworld. He was the seventh mage, the most powerful mage. And now he will not live to realise his full potential. And what was he doing in here in the first place?'

'I believe I had something to do with that,' muttered Tweak.

Marl turned to regard the little dwarf. They all regarded him.

'And who are you exactly?'

The little dwarf started to look worried and with good reason.

'I'm Tweak, chief magician…chief jester to the house of René. I…I followed Fabian here as he was instrumental in the disappearance of the ambassador of the pioneers of Sinistrom sovereignty, and…'

'Are you accusing this man of something, dwarf?' Justas Marl spoke as he was beginning to take offence.

'Accusing?' Tweak answered, beginning to feel as though he was on trial for everything that had just happened. 'I saw his alter ego. I saw the dragon rise, create terror in the streets, billowing flames, if you please! I saw the dragon snatch the ambassador from the ground and damn near—'

'Hold your tongue!' Marl spoke fiercely, crouching before the little man so that their eyes were level. 'Did you actually see the kidnapping? Did you actually see Fabian take the ambassador? Did you see it, Dwarf?'

'Yes!' Tweak tried to back away, but his passage was blocked by Draethor who was standing directly behind him.

'I saw the dragon with my own eyes!' he stammered.

'No.' Corrected the mage. 'I didn't ask you whether you saw the dragon or not. My question to you was, did you see Fabian? Do not play games with me today, dwarf!'

Justas Marl turned away and stopped. He was beginning to lose his patience with the small-minded dwarf.

'I asked you who you saw.' The tall man calmed his voice, though it was still knotted with certain grief.

'I told you, I saw the dragon,' Tweak answered, frustrated.

The taller man turned on his heels and crouched once again before the dwarf.

'And that is why you saw only what the enemy wished you to see. You didn't witness Fabian take the ambassador at all!'

'What are you talking about? You're mad.' Tweak accused the tall man.

Marl fought back the impulse to simply lock his bare hands around the dwarf's gullet and squeeze the life from the imbecilic little yokel.

'I am talking about an enemy that can change himself and mimic any form, any shape he desires, even a dragon. I am talking about an enemy that wanted to discredit the prince in order to start a war between the people of Mundor and the Sinistrom. I am saying, if you'd just take those cotton balls out your flaming ears and listen, that that corpse lying there tried very hard and came all this distance to try and rescue the ambassador and avert war!'

Tweak noticed the tall man pull a knife from its sheath, and then felt its cold metal against his bare throat.

'It has taken us a long time to find the seventh mage! That would be five decades, 52 long years to be exact. Give me a reason why I shouldn't gut you right now.'

A bright light glared in their faces suddenly, brighter

than the brightest sun. The seven individuals shielded their eyes.

Marl felt the knife slip from his grasp. The light vanished quickly and in its place there was a blue dragon, and definitely not the same fiery red creature they had seen previously.

'By the ancients,' whispered Marl, unable to believe his eyes.

Before them stood a Loch Water Dragon, similar in appearance and size to the one which Fabian had turned into on that previous encounter, only this one was a different hue entirely.

'It makes perfect sense,' said Iron May, realising the ingenuity of it. 'He adapted to his imminent drowning by becoming a Loch Water Dragon.'

'It is true,' remarked Marl, taking a few steps towards the large creature standing before them. 'Loch Water Dragons are at home in mystic waters, probably explains how he was able to survive for as long as he did in those falls. He has the ability to adapt to every danger. Inspired!'

The dragon splayed its webbed wings apart and instantly took flight. The ceiling of the grotto broke and shattered as the powerful beast burst through solid rock in a bid to escape this subterranean world. No mere confinement would ever imprison this free and uninhibited spirit again! The mages quickly scrambled to safety as rock and dust fell and billowed, filling the cavern around them.

Topside, the dragon stood majestically under the sight of the moon and stars before changing back into the boy they all thought to be dead.

'I did it!' The boy announced, weeping tears of joy, and looking down at his hands, his human hands. He looked up only to see Marl, his new friend and teacher, approaching him with his arms open wide.

He embraced the young prince. Tweak looked on, both relieved that his old friend was still alive, yet gripped by remorse that he had judged his friend and prince wrongly, and had treated him with not only suspicion, but prejudice as well.

'We thought we'd lost you.' Marl wept, embracing Fabian. 'My brother...I thought I had.'

Brother. This was unexpected, though welcoming. Fabian had never had any siblings.

Yes, brother sounded good.

Chapter 11

Cougar Chuko looked up at the mass of flesh, sinew, and fangs that was chained to the metal bulkhead. It seemed tame, for the moment anyway, tranquilised for the protection of the guards and owners that came to care and tend to its every desire. Standing over thirty feet tall, it lurched sleepily in its manmade cage while Chuko's two right hand men tried to keep it still with long support rods.

'He'll be hungry in a few hours.' Observed the Cougar, confidently, his hands clasped behind his back. 'Tonight's menu boasts a truly inspired dish I like to call, Mort a˘ la Ambassador.'

He kissed the tips of his fingers as he finished by saying: 'It truly is to die for.'

The early sun was barely visible on the horizon. Tweak looked up at his former friend. The little guy was finding it difficult to express his guilty feelings. Finally, he said:

'I'm sorry. I'm sorry for everything. When I saw that dragon in the marketplace...When I saw it carry the ambassador off to the gods know what hellish destination, and after I'd seen you transform into that...'

'How did you see that?' the prince interrupted. 'How, Tweak, when I never let anyone see my gift and transformation?'

Marl, who was near enough to overhear the conversation betwixt the two, discerned the word "gift" used instead of the word "curse". This made Marl smile.

'I guess I was being a bit of a busybody as usual,' Tweak said with much embarrassment. 'I called upon the reflection of a magic mirror. It revealed to me the truth of why you suddenly ran away, and why the king had you dragged back wrapped in a blanket. It was all rather suspicious. What the mirror showed me was unbelievable, but the mirror never lies. I could neither deny nor forget what I'd seen. The mirror showed me you in the woods, saving a child from a carnivorous pitcher plant. I chose to ignore that good deed in favour of the transformation that miraculously took place. The dragon in the marketplace was identical to you, that is the dragon you become.'

'So, what changed your mind about me? Why apologise to me if you think I am evil?'

'I don't think you're evil. I heard Marl say that a trickster was responsible for taking your dragon's form, and that it was this trickster that spirited away the ambassador—not you. I understand now that I was wrong. This has been some terrible misunderstanding. Please, I'm sorry.'

Fabian witnessed the tears forming in the dwarf's eyes, and thought that he had made him suffer long enough. He had obviously learnt his lesson.

The sun was finally up over the desert. The seven travellers, accompanied by Tweak, continued on their journey. The trail had gone dead a while ago. Fortunately, Tweak had some experience with tracking spells. His knowledge would be of immeasurable value in the continued quest.

He knelt on a flat bed of dry earth and unfolded a small piece of material that was no larger than a handkerchief. Upon the material he placed a sharpened stone and two other, more polished stones, next to it. These stones had strange symbols engraved on them. He said a mantra, and instantly the stones began to move by themselves.

'Show me where the Sinistrom ambassador can be found.' He commanded.

The sharpened stone in the middle began to vibrate, and then tilt upwards towards the sky on its own. Tweak looked up, puzzled.

'Why, according to this stone the ambassador is…up there!'

They all looked up.

'That's impossible!' Draethor exclaimed.

'Not necessarily.' Prompted Tweak, remembering his mythology. 'Some dragons have been known to sleep amidst the clouds. Clouds can be cradles to those that know the ways of magic.'

'Do you know the way?' Justas Marl asked the dwarf.

'Of course, I do! I am a magician, you know. Alright, I am just a humble fool, but I am well versed in magic!'

Tweak said another mantra and, in a heartbeat, a rather sizeable cloud sailed down from the sky and alighted at their feet.

'All aboard!' the dwarf said, spryly, stepping onto the cloud.

'You're not getting me on that!' Draethor exclaimed, folding his arms.

'It's perfectly safe.' Tweak assured him.

'I'll stay here if it's all the same to you!'

The dwarf muttered under his breath, 'Move your sissy ass.'

The cloud rose, lifting Tweak and the remaining six mages higher into the ether. Above all other cloud, they matched stature with the heavens. As the white patterns of veil and nimbus gave way suddenly to blue sky they witnessed a sight completely alien to them: a city—a city in the air. It was simply hovering there like a bird. *This isn't magic*, Tweak thought, *this was something else, not new, but old, older than magic, older than myth…this is science!*

This was Urban Cloud, the hidden city of the Head Hunters.

'Is there any way in?' asked the dwarf, looking for some kind of opening.

Justas Marl suggested that they look around the underside. There had to be some kind of access. It was a city and, like all cities, there were pipes, ducts, entrance tunnels, that sort of thing. Maybe there was a way in large enough for a cloud and seven people to enter.

'There!' Colonel Warclaw pointed.

The others gazed upon the immense size of the levitating city. An aperture opened suddenly, and green slime and water filtered out, sending waste and refuse away over the sky as though a cloud had just burst. It was foul smelling. Tweak pinched his nose and held his breath. The six mages almost got the full brunt of it, but the deluge veered off to the side with the force of the wind.

'That's our access point,' Marl said.

'You have to be joking.' Katt Brutal criticised, holding her nose.

In they went, into the rear of the sky-worthy leviathan, into the ductwork and up, before finally reaching the plumbing. They had abandoned their wispy mode of transportation and had taken to crawling through the network of piping before reaching an access to the main command deck. A grating in the floor's plating lifted up and a head emerged. It was Marl's head. He looked around to see the last occupant of the room leave. The coast was clear. They climbed up from the vent, one after the other.

'We'll need some kind of internal map or something.' Iron May suggested, looking around the corner into the next corridor. Katt, who was small and lithe, leapt like a gymnast and began to scramble across the ceiling with the dexterity of a spider or a monkey. She was gone before the others could object.

'Come on!' Marl ordered the others. 'It'll do us no good if she gets herself captured.'

The rest of the party followed Marl's lead through a series of corridors. This place had to be immense. There were many rooms on board the command level, all of which were manned by officers and Head Hunters. It was hazardous to be wandering about in these spaces without any idea of where they were going. Suddenly, the alarms sounded and the mages that were left were surrounded in an instant. Soldiers entered, flooding into the tiny space, their guns focused on the intruders.

Marl and the others lifted their arms in surrender.

Cougar Chuko was at the head of his security team.

'Mages,' Chuko said, rubbing his fur lined chin thoughtfully. 'You would have to be mages, wouldn't you? You are the people on this backwater world capable of reaching this city in the sky. It was all for naught anyway, as you will soon discover.'

Chuko turned to his lieutenant.

'I want the other one found immediately. Take as many hunters and troops as you need, but find her.'

'Yes, master. At once,' the lieutenant said.

The creature moved away, pulling his gun from his holster. The hunt was on.

Katt was swift, darting through the ship, covering more distance alone than she would have if she had stayed with her companions. *At times, impetuosity is an advantage*, she thought. Through the ductwork and tiny spaces she crawled. There were indeed places, corners in this vast and unparalleled city, that Katt had never imagined, not even in her remotest imaginings. Worlds beyond worlds; rooms, conduits which would lead to a thousand other possibilities…There were literally billions upon billions of spaces and existences that would make even the world from which she had come look tame and commonplace.

Katt emerged from the small grate. She then chose a direction and decided to follow it. Entering the next room in the traditional way, which was to say, vertically, Katt discovered the next adjacent room was a complete contrast in decorative style to the last one she had entered. What a spectacle of slender columns greeted her eyes. Searching upwards, tilting her head, Katt saw the magnificent circular paintings stretching out along the entablature. Complete frescos, portraits of heroes, gods, and goddesses, wallowing in lavishness, circled the length of these spaces like a story being told in pictures. The wonderful black and white fret patterns on the tiled floor, the golden architrave—all these designs Katt barely recognised.

After taking in the sights, she moved to the adjoining room and here she was greeted by a circular area with a single flight of stairs. The landing at the top of the stairs began to section off in either direction, making the introduction to a circular stairwell that began to stretch upwards, so it seemed, without end. Katt was utterly breath taken.

She ascended the staircase quietly, slowly taking in all the delicate fixtures and shades of the colours gold and emerald. There were beautiful balustrades, iron sconces, and extremely narrow pilasters between which paintings or mirrors were positioned. Suddenly, she noticed a human shape in the distance, some flights up. She saw the form of a man or some such creature dressed in grey robes. The voice that spoke sliced through the tense calm:

'Stop her! Fire your weapons!'

As the guards accompanied the prisoners to the detention wing, Justas Marl called upon his bird tattoo to warn Katt of the contingency. The bright golden artwork that adorned the soft tissue of his face began to flutter and flap gracefully. In an astonishing display of enchantment, ink separated from flesh, flapping its imaginary wings, flying straight in a direct line towards the bulkhead. Passing through the wall, the magical tattoo made all haste to where Katt was positioned.

One of the guards, upon witnessing this magic trick,

turned and jammed the butt of his rifle into the back of Marl's neck. The mage fell to the ground unconscious with a loud groan.

'Pick that up.' The man ordered his subordinate. 'I'll have no more of that augury here!'

The guard approached and collected the mage, lifting him up and then carrying him the rest of the way.

'There,' the guard said blockishly to the prisoners that were still very much conscious. 'A nice prison cell for each of you. Hope you all get dry rot. You're going to be here a while.'

The guards burst into laughter as they busied themselves, ushering their guests into their respective cages. And that is all they were: cages unfit even for animals.

A small stubby creature, resembling something like a flea or termite, gurgled and chortled aloud, it's dozens of tiny, larvae-like mandibles skittered and writhed. The unsightly creature wore a leather apron and appeared to be holding a pair of metal tongs or tweezers down, partially submerged in a small vat of chemicals.

The guards turned to the creature before leaving the victims to their fate:

'Make sure our guests are comfortable, Vorm. That's a good man!'

The guards left the room laughing boisterously.

Fabian, who had been goaded into a large birdcage suspended by a steel cable from the ceiling, could not help but notice the little man they had called Vorm, who was beginning to prepare his implements of torture.

The bird tattoo searched for Katt. It examined deck after deck until it came across a stairwell. The stairs seemed to spiral in either direction forever, though there were sounds, sounds of angry voices directly below that alerted the magical tattoo bird to the immediate danger. Maybe it was too late to warn Katt.

'Stop her!' Came the voices in the distance. 'Fire your weapons!'

The command was followed by a barrage of heavy fire, all of which Katt was able to avoid. The tattoo bird plunged down the stairwell, down to the very epicentre where the action was taking place. It circled the heads of the soldiers, drawing their fire long enough for the lithe little Katt to escape.

'You fools!' Reprimanded the lieutenant. 'Send the hunter in after her! Go! Go!'

Katt and the bird both covered quite a substantial distance together. The cat-like mage was fast, darting from room to room, and then vanishing, and appearing mischievously for a moment, only to evaporate mysteriously again.

These stairs seemed to spiral on upwards forever.

Finally, the mage stopped before a door and looked behind to see if she was still being followed by Head Hunters. Then, with a wily little smile, she vanished and was gone from sight.

The Head Hunter's shouts were perfectly audible, even from a distance, though there was no fixed position to pinpoint the sounds. Katt entered the room, searching this way and then that. This place appeared to be a gallery of some kind, an extended room with an endless chain of rooms beyond, separated by simple round arches and decorated with landscape paintings and various portraits.

It suddenly occurred to her that this city was not merely a city, but an entire universe, infinite in measure. Each room was like a magical portal to another world. An infinite number of magical portals laced these corridors, all doorways to other rooms, other worlds, infinite in number, Labyrinthine and inestimable. The architectural genius it must have taken to conceive of this infinite place. Room upon room, upon room, upon room…endless! It grew upwards and outwards like a tree, branching, lateral. It was an immeasurable world fashioned for the sake of longevity perhaps, like a story told by Scheherazade. Why, this was not a universe of comets or stars, or gas giants, or space debris. There were no inhabited planets and no suns. There were only billions upon billions of galleries, never-ending stairs, and quarters. It was dizzying. The mind could not stretch to such possibilities.

Behind her the violent shouts of 'Deploy the hunter! Find her!' could be discerned.

Katt slipped away, out of sight.

One room followed another, and then another, and another, until she reached an attached wing veering to the right and to the left. Katt was beginning to feel worried. What if she could never find her way back again? What if she ended up losing her way? The thought of this was terrifying.

There was another door directly to her side. She turned, entering swiftly. She glanced behind momentarily to check the progress of her pursuers, only to vanish again. The tattoo bird could sense an ambush. Cautiously, Katt entered the room.

Another chamber greeted her with its walls coated in stucco, with niches decorated with busts and statues. Marble pillars adorned the outer area with plinths cut to the neat profile of many plumes.

Katt scanned the room from top to bottom. There was no sign of another door by which she could make a swift exit. There had to be something though. There was no such thing as a cul de sac where this city was concerned. It didn't make any sense.

Something didn't feel right. Katt got the strange sense that she had been goaded into entering this room.

She turned around, looking to find anything that might have indicated a way out, a secret trapdoor, anything. She turned repeatedly on her feet. The walls were like a spinning carousel. The feeling was unsettling. It was like being caught in some kind of dimensional shift. There appeared a door, suddenly, but not a conventional door. There was no lintel or framework, only momentary lapses of time, a discreet reallocation of matter. Before she knew what had happened she had been transported, molecule by molecule, to another part of the city.

Katt found herself unexpectedly standing in a very different place. She saw a tall throne made of shining gold. A rather high and elegant man rose from a luxuriously upholstered seat and was on his feet the second Katt caught sight of him. The stranger wore a golden mask over his face, intricate in pattern and Machiavellian in purpose. It was accentuated and framed by a design similar to a cobra's outstretched hood. The creature looked intently back at her with shrewd eyes that were heavily piercing, drawn behind the subtle shaded sockets of that burnished mask. His skin revealed many scales as if he was more reptile than man.

'Who are you? What is your name?' The man who resembled an ancient potentate suddenly inquired. His words were in a strange dialect which Katt could barely understand.

She stood in stunned silence, not knowing how dangerous he was.

'May I ask what you are doing here?' the other asked again.

When Katt did not answer, the stranger said, 'Well...? You come into my universe uninvited and unannounced. Who are you? Pray, why are you here? Answer me!'

As his anger and fury rose from the trough of his diaphragm he was instantly joined by another man, if a man is what you could call him. For like the being that had spoken, he too had reptilian features. Katt, however, recognised this creature straight away. Fear rose in her as she was able to make out the faction and division to which he and his reptilian brethren belonged. This vile creature was none other than Cotton Jaw, one of Malecarjan's snake hunters. As one appeared, another followed from behind the throne. This one wore a long, flowing trench coat and an old tri-corn hat. His face was fully elongated, and his mouth was full of rows of serrated teeth. He was acknowledged as Coachwhip. Then another warrior came into full view, followed by yet another, and another. These three were known primarily as Hook-nose, Saw Scale, and The Black Monda. Three very dangerous snakes indeed.

The one who had appeared first, the creature standing directly before the throne, reached up with a clawed hand to activate the mask he was wearing. The golden and intricately carved visor gave a small but audible hissing sound as it parted slowly in the centre nomenclature, and then lifting steadily of its own mechanics to reveal a real face, a scaly, alien face which Katt now recognised. This was their general, the fearless Aspasian.

Katt began to back away slowly, knowing full well she was well and truly in trouble.

'Why do you not answer?' Aspasian demanded, losing his patience. 'I'll ask you again: what are you doing here?'

Katt continued to back away. She was almost to the door.

'Do you know where you are?' the general challenged.

Again, Katt did not answer. After all, she had a rough idea.

'This is the world of science and mystery.' Malecarjan's general aimed to enlighten her. 'This is the world that created us, the viper masters. If I was to give you a history, I would say that this is the world from whence we came, now very much shattered, fractured, and timeless. We were born here. We were raised here as our masters used its technology to reach your world. It is run by scavengers now, but it is still where it all began. Right here in this forge.'

The mage continued to step backwards. The general began to take a series of large steps toward her also. His enormous red robes swirled and danced around his feet as he moved. He began to pick up speed with every stride.

The snake known as Coachwhip whirled his powerful cat-o-nine-tails above his head and brought it swiftly to the floor that made a piercing thwack upon the marble.

Cotton Jaw merely stood his ground, dislocated his jaw like an anaconda, and spat out fine threads from the back of his throat. Much akin to a spider spinning a web, he hurled the threads in Katt's direction hoping to ensnare her in his many strands.

Katt, with her great agility, managed to evade the attack.

"Answer me! Who are you? Why did you come here?" Aspasian continued while he sustained his pursuit. 'You can run, but against my power you are helpless to evade capture!'

Katt continued to look on, alarmed, fearful of what she saw. It only took a split second; Aspasian was changing, not only in appearance, but in bulk and stature as well. Katt was well aware of this creature's powers as she and her companions had faced his likes before and knew that Aspasian was a shape shifter. She watched helplessly as the transformation began. Muscles and sinews swelled, undulating, heaving under the camouflage of skin. Veins as thick as rope surged beneath the layers of flesh, like dark and bloody cables. In spite of his reptilian appearance, the general began to simulate mammalian qualities: thick hair developed over his muscles and spread over his body. The transformation was swift and terrible. It was a kind of lycanthropy over a snake-like predator. The creature who was once Malecarjan's second in command quickly removed and discarded the golden mask, revealing the face of a vicious snake creature like nothing Katt had seen before. Its teeth bore down as it snivelled and howled. The body of a great hound was followed by the tail that emerged with the head of a snake at one end. Half-hound, half serpent, he had become a nightmare.

Katt turned on her heels and ran. The tattoo bird followed, making its warning cry.

The monster lurched forward, going down on all fours. It barked and rasped. Red eyes, eyes that once appeared human, bore down on its prey.

"Come here!" it snarled. "You cannot flee the death!"

It howled and barked, demonstrating the grey madness of a soul that believed and trusted nothing. It bayed for Katt's suffering. Its footfalls were laboured, though they sounded like dull thunderbolts on the marble floor.

Chapter 12

There was very little time for torture or fun. No sooner had the jailer taken his tongs out of the acid vat when Cougar Chuko returned with fresh orders. He gestured towards Fabian in his hanging birdcage.

'The one hanging up there is to be transferred to the arena immediately. Have him change and sent directly to the circus master to be processed. The others are not to be harmed, you understand?'

Chuko left the room more quickly than he had entered. The freakish little jailer shot a quick expletive in the direction of the door and dropped the tongs back into the vat with a sharp and bothered thrust of his stubby hand.

Fabian turned his attentions to the guard, and then to the keys he was shuffling about in his gloved hands. Heavens be praised, he was actually going to be let out.

'Don't start gettin' your hopes up,' the guard muttered in a thuggish tone as he placed the appropriate key in the lock. 'You're goin' to wish you'd stayed here under

Vorm's tender mercy rather than face the ordeal that awaits you, my young friend.'

The cage door swung open.

'Out you come!'

Fabian squeezed out of the bird cage and felt relieved to stretch his legs again after being cooped up.

'Circus? Wait, what arena? You can't do this to me. I'm a peer of the realm. Stop. Unhand me!' The prince ordered as he was goaded to the exit. The other mages watched helplessly.

'Oh pardon me, Your Lordship.' The guard gave a brief, but humorous curtsy. 'Now keep yur flamin' trap shut!'

Fabian was ushered to a distant section of the city. The style of each room seemed to alter considerably. The walls, ceilings, and floors of the command level seemed to be composed of metal and futuristic materials, while other rooms were built from stone blocks and were rough and extremely dusty. There was sand underfoot. Fabian quickly noted this as he moved through these poorly lit spaces. *What is this place?* The boy could not help but be overwhelmed by the question, by the size and inconsistency of the city. *Is this magic? Is it something older? Is this science?*

'Come on!' The guard instructed. 'We have to fit you up. You're going to get a nice new suit of amour. The Maumothax likes his food to put up a bit of a fight before he devours them whole.'

Fabian stopped at the doorway and looked at the guard behind him.

'Go on! Stop dawdling.'

The guard pushed the prince into the adjoining room.

It was a wide, circular area. Several sturdy wooden racks were positioned along the circumference. One rack held spears of various lengths. Another held swords and other stabbing weapons. There were javelins, spiked weapons, maces, even guns of varying detail and design. This had to be an armory. Fabian felt a chill suddenly as the realisation struck him.

There was a helmet as well as arm and leg guards, and a breast plate waiting for him. The deluge remained on the dusty floor.

'Put them on!'

Fabian did as he was told. Uncertainly, he placed the helmet over his head first and then commenced to put the breast plate straps over his shoulders.

The guard's brow tightened with annoyance.

As Fabian leant forwards his helmet slid off. Then

awkwardly he let go of the chest guard before he had even secured the straps around his waist.

'Where did you learn to dress yourself?' the guard said.

He dashed forwards to pick the breast plate and helmet off the floor.

'Put the guards on your arms and legs first. Then the breast plate and helmet afterwards. Got it?'

Fabian felt humiliated, but he did as he was told.

Eventually he was ready to confront whatever hell they were going to put him through. He selected a weapon, a machete from one of the racks.

Impatiently the guard spurred him on, urging him into an adjoining room.

Fabian could not believe the sight that greeted him.

Sounds of thunder seemed to emanate from the vast arena, filtering through into the tiny quarters where the ambassador sat dejectedly. His hands were bound with metal restraints. He could hear the rumble of the mob clearly from where he was. Tears began to trickle down his face. He looked up as he gave in to sobs. It was clear that this room was an antechamber between the armoury and whatever awaited him out there.

The ambassador was waiting for the end to come.

He looked across at the door he had recently entered. His face lit up like a lively torch flame as he watched Prince Fabian being escorted into the room. He would have leapt up out of his seat were it not for the chains that linked his restraints to the stone wall.

Fabian, however, was less restrained at that moment and moved to embrace his lover.

'I came here to find you.' The prince wept tears of relief and joy.

'I'm so glad you're here.' It was all Tør could say.

'Touching,' said the guard, mockingly. 'Well, any minute now you are going to enjoy a nice romantic meal together. Two delectable morsels such as yourselves would make the night really special. The table's been set, the candle's been lit, a little music to help get in the mood…Now let's see how fast you darling lovers can run.'

The guard laughed loudly as he snatched Fabian by the arm, parting him from the hands of the ambassador.

The place shook as one footfall followed another. Katt looked back over her shoulder as the immense creature quickened its pace to match. It lunged with all its weight, charging like a bull, bursting and tearing through partitions with all its inhuman strength and resolve.

Its hideous cry sounded, giving Katt chills.

The mage turned sharply and made her hasty retreat through the gallery of pictures. Clumsily, the beast pounced, crashing to the floor in an awkward heap.

It soon shook off its confusion and began the pursuit again.

Katt looked back over her shoulder. *I'm not out of the woods yet*, she thought, picking up speed.

Pictures swayed and tilted, or fell, scattering shards of glass everywhere.

Luckily, the cat-like mage succeeded in making it to the stairwell at the end of the hall.

Down the stairs she ran, her feet treading hastily as she negotiated each step. That monstrous thing burst through the partitions, straight through marble and stone as though the walls were made of paper.

Stone and plaster flew everywhere. The scattering debris tumbled, ending with a dull clattering sound as it hit the marble floor so far below. The creature hurled itself at Katt, using the iron banisters to swing from level to level like a limber simian. It was gaining ground fast.

Katt thought little of the danger. She had to gain

some distance and quick. Swiftly, she lifted her foot up onto the banister and hoisted herself up…over she went.

The creature lunged at its prey, barely missing its intended target.

Katt began to free-fall. She swam through the air like a bullet, down through the centre of this winding stairwell. The mage plunged, holding her arms out to try to catch one of the banisters as she made her descent. She managed to grasp one, but as her hands gripped it tightly, her body slammed mightily against the side of the stair. A sudden cry of pain echoed upwards from the epicentre as the creature jumped from banister to banister, following the sounds his victim made.

The creature was above her, descending fast. It clawed with its muscular arms and slender fingers, fingers that tapered into sharp-edged claws.

Katt's grip steadily slackened from the pain in her upper arm. She could not hold on any longer, and started to fall again.

She tried to brace herself with her arms flung out before her, then became conscious of the fact that cats always landed squarely on their feet, and would likely survive a fall like this, even with a compromised shoulder.

It was as Katt surmised. She had landed on her feet

and hands. Quickly, she scrambled out of the way just as the great beast came crashing down. There was a loud thud and then no sound at all. The immense bulk lay dead and motionless in the centre of the floor.

Katt watched the blood dribble from the fresh carcass of the beast. The pool was getting larger and wider as it spilled out onto the marble floor.

Rapidly, the feral, fur lined face began to morph back into a human shape. Katt recognised the reptilian countenance. It was Aspasian. But he was not dead, merely immobile. That she soon discovered as the tiny serpent-like heads began to poke through the bloodied and open wound of the man lying prostrate. He was regenerating, casting off the huge husk as though it was merely useless skin. The snakes emerged further into view and began to slither off in all directions, leaving a trail of blood side winding along the floor. Katt began to back away while the serpents took to the shadows and the cracks in the walls. They would require little time to merge together and to restore themselves fully.

It was almost unbearable, the roar of the crowd as the two prisoners entered the arena. There had been nothing like this in the whole of Mundorian history, at least nothing that remained on documented record. This was truly barbaric.

Fabian and Tør remained overwhelmed as they watched the throng, the sick, the twisted, and the social cretin, all in the mix who had paid a pretty penny to come watch the slaughter. Many bashed their fists upon the stalls, sending up a terrible rhythm that filled their ears.

The arena, a large, circular sandpit, had not been cleared since the previous games. This was obvious since there were vestiges of corpses lying on the ground: gladiatorial leftovers from a previous battle. There were also traps as well as devices set up to aid the victim and give him a fighting chance. In the distance there appeared to be a raised platform or ramp. Maybe the ramp was a means for the victim to gain high ground when needed. It seemed likely that their captors would wish them to put up a good fight for the entertainment of the mob before they died.

Cougar Chuko, accompanied by a slave girl, sat beneath a raised canopy gloating like a fat Caesar at the head of the mob.

'Release the Maumothax!' Commanded Chuko.

Upon this command the crowds roared even more loudly than before. The sound of metal chains clinking directed the attentions of the two victims as they watched a large, rusty grating slide upwards, revealing a dark and forbidding tunnel in the corner of the arena. The mob went silent suddenly, replaced by the rapid bloodcurdling, thunderous cry of something very large.

Swiftly, Fabian felt an inadequacy in the weapon he was holding. The machete he had chosen from the armoury fell from his grip. There were other weapons littered along the ground, he noted. Or he could simply become the dragon again. All this could be over in a heartbeat, but no. To call forth the Tolan would have meant revealing his duality to Tør. That would have been unconscionable. Finally, Fabian bent down to retrieve a metal trident, a sturdy enough weapon with plenty of distance end to end. At that point he felt a little more confident to greet the horror that was about to present itself. Likewise, the ambassador slowly picked up a tiny sickle and net. Between the two of them, he was the one who felt the least protected.

They both stepped back a few paces. The sound of a large animal could be heard by its would-be victims. Two or three loud snorts from the unseen beast in the darkness gave one the impression it, whatever it was, could smell the fear of the two humans in the showground.

There was a short uneasy pause and then, without warning, the creature exploded from the tunnel. It was built like a silverback gorilla but was at least 3 times the size with a greyish pelt and strong forearms.

The ambassador fell backwards. Fabian had a clear shot to the side of the creature's neck. He took his opportunity and buried the trident into the creature's fur-lined pelt. The Maumothax bawled out in pain and turned its head, knocking the prince to the ground with a thrust of its massive arm. The ambassador, realising the attentions of the creature had moved to Fabian, decided to make his move. He climbed up onto a raised platform and then pounced on the monster's back. Okay, so the tiny net was going to be of little use to him, and the sickle might have proven to be as effective as a spear made of cardboard, still, he hadn't really given it much thought.

The beast bucked and tried to dodge the human hanging onto its back for dear life. The crowd was amused and so was Chuko, who sat and watched the spectacle with abysmal glee.

Katt watched the two guards from her vantage point on the ceiling. Her long tail was wrapped around a pipe as she hung there. The duct's metal surface felt warm against her skin. The two guards, who were securing the prisoners, were completely oblivious to her presence.

Katt had a plan. Moving like a dart, she clung to the head of one of the guards and licked his face. The other guard raised his rifle to attack the intruder. Katt looked round at him, thumbed her nose disrespectfully and stuck her tongue out. The guard gritted his teeth and began to squeeze on the trigger. She leaped clean out of harm's way just as the gun went off. The resultant blast made a clean hole where the other guard's face used to be. The man with the rifle was left wincing at the damage. That was when Katt came back round and sank her sharp teeth into his leather crotch, bringing a spate of tears to his eyes.

This brought the guard to his knees, holding his injured scrotum with both hands.

Quickly, Katt removed the key chain from his belt and moved to free her companions from their respective cells. Justas Marl, of course, had been alerted ten minutes earlier to Katt's arrival. His tattoo bird had returned, adhering itself to the side of his face. When Katt asked how he knew, Marl simply replied:

'A little bird told me.' And then tapped the right

hemisphere of his face where the tattoo sat with his index finger and winked at her.

The Maumothax bucked suddenly, throwing the ambassador from its back. The boy lay there silent where he had fallen, unconscious.

Fabian was roused suddenly. Quickly noticing the small cube-like object on the floor next to him, Fabian recalled that he had placed the holographic projector that belonged to Tør in his pocket. It must have rolled out as he fell, he reasoned as he snatched the device from the ground.

The terrible Maumothax held its ground before the boy. It snorted, dragging its foot in the sand like a bull before making its charge.

It began to stampede. Its mighty muscles rippled beneath its hairy pelt as it neared the helpless boy.

Pressing the switch on the small holographic device, Fabian hurled it at the great beast, throwing it completely off balance. That was nothing however compared to the disorientation it felt as the device activated, emitting a blinding light. The creature howled out in fear, unsettled by the holograms that were suddenly emitted, altering the very nature and appearance of the arena and the world surrounding it. Unable to comprehend what it was seeing, it bayed and barked like a frightened animal. Remarkably, the Eiffel Tower appeared surrounded by a great open space, trees, fountains, people—an alien environment of strange and incredible wonders! Paris loomed in all directions, taking shape, fading out all evidence of the arena. It was all rather implausible, but there it was. These holograms appeared from all sides.

The beast looked this way and that, trying to make sense of what it was seeing. Even the vast audience rose from the seats and began to chatter with much confusion. Chuko also got out of his seat. He could not see the holograms, but he could sense there was a slight distortion surrounding the creature in the arena. He shouted instructions to put an end to this disruption immediately.

Closing his eyes and believing in his true power, Fabian decided that the moment was right to call upon the help of his alter ego. He began the transformation into the Dragon Tolan.

Cougar Chuko's expression changed dramatically, witnessing the impossible sight. The dragon stood before the mob and at that moment the spectators' shouts faded to a silence.

The Maumothax thundered, thumping its fists on the turf irritably. The holographic cube was quickly crushed under the weight of the monster. In an instant the arena returned, and the Paris facsimile vanished. It no longer mattered. The Dragon Tolan slowly raised one clawed hand, showing the Maumothax its index finger and motioned as if to say, "Come and get me".

The Maumothax seemed only too happy to oblige. Kicking up tons of sand with its back legs, it prepared to charge its new enemy. It thundered across the arena, snorting like a bull. The Dragon Tolan inhaled a generous amount of air and then let rip. Plumes of fire spewed from its mouth. The Maumothax was caught suddenly, unable to stop in time, and was almost incinerated.

The ambassador stirred, becoming conscious, finally. He looked up and witnessed the Maumothax fighting another monster, a great winged dragon, and wondered if he was still dreaming. The dragon, however, was extremely familiar: the large webbed hood that fanned outwards from its head, the vermilion eyes, and the face—it was the same dragon that had abducted him in the marketplace! He was certain of it. And here it was, saving their lives from this terrible brutish creature... But what had happened to Fabian in all of this chaos? Was he dead? Had he been vanquished? Tør hoped to the gods this wasn't so.

Katt had sprung the other mages, though escape was proving to be difficult. One of the guards hit the alarms just as another one of Chuko's men, a cybernetic creature known as Mugshot, moved into the room gradually, clanking like a slow-moving tin can.

This was a Head Hunter with a mean streak. Half man, half robot, he moved in ahead of the assembly of guards, parting them with his hands.

'Steady,' it said, with a grave, robotic tone. 'Leave these miscreants to me. I'll deal with them.'

The mages noticed the odd creature known as Mugshot, the steel armour that he wore, almost similar to that of a knight's but with wires and tubes accentuated around every curvature of metal.

'Transform!' He thundered in a mechanical manner. 'Transform! Fire! Fire!'

Marl and the other mages began to back away.

'Over there.' Centorionn pointed in the direction of a raised metal structure. 'Run!'

The mages darted for cover.

The cyborg transformed itself into its cannon mode. Its head was about to detach like a separate projectile.

'Fire now!'

The head lunged from its main body. The bulkhead exploded above the mage's heads, raining metal and debris down on top of them. Mugshot reloaded.

His second head emerged, ready and primed. It volleyed from the barrel, detonating along the bulkhead, blocking the mage's getaway. Mugshot quickly transformed back into a humanoid again.

'No escape. You're coming with us,' said the bombastic Mugshot. Another third head emerged to replace the other two that had been spent.

One of the guards advanced on the mages, taking hand restraints from his belt to fit each of them.

Tweak, who had been standing behind the other mages, slowly reached into his service belt and removed a small smoke pellet.

There was a sharp sound like glass breaking, and then the dense shroud of grey smoke filled the corridor.

'Hurry!' Marl commanded, taking this opportunity to escape. In the confusion Centorionn managed to deliver a rather heavy cloven hoof which landed squarely upon Mugshot's foot, the resulting effect was his third head lunging from his neck like a cannon ball only to bury itself in the ceiling above. The severed head was lodged, unable to move.

'Oh, no,' the decapitated head said with dismay. 'Not again!'

The resulting explosion forced half the upper level to collapse in on top of Mugshot's body. This creature, that could turn himself into a mortar at will, was buried under tons of debris finally.

The other Head Hunters had drawn their pistols and began blasting away at the thick smoke, hoping to hit something. They did. They hit a gas main and the whole room exploded, sending other Head Hunters reeling backwards onto the rubble.

As the mages escaped onto the next level they heard another explosion. It was obvious this section was becoming unstable. They hurried, making their way up many flights of stairs before they came to another prisoner cell block. Before them was a stockpile of weapons, spears, swords, maces, as well as various suits of armour and helmets. There were even gladiatorial helmets which strongly indicated that there must have been some kind of showground nearby.

Grabbing a weapon each, the mages hurried along a dark corridor, which led them eventually to a large metal grating. The sounds of battle could be discerned beyond. With a slight prestidigitation, Tweak managed to raise the grating using a little magic. As the mages strolled into the arena they recognised the Dragon Tolan instantly and another monster, obviously somewhat subdued. The dragon held the creature upside down and then began to swing its body round by its left leg, round and round and round, picking up speed, before letting go. The Maumothax was hurled into the crowd, and the crowd dispersed in a panic to escape.

Cougar Chuko was on his feet and was already calling for his guards. The side of the stadium erupted into flame as the great beast landed. The bloodthirsty spectators were all extinguished in a split second. The rest of the throng absconded. People were falling on the ground as others, in a mad bid to discharge themselves, stepped on them and trod their bones into t he earth.

His wrath abating, the Dragon Tolan transformed back into a boy. Fortunately, the ambassador did not witness the change in time. In the confusion, he looked and saw Fabian standing there, and mysteriously the dragon was gone.

'What happened?' the confused emissary asked. 'I saw a dragon appear...It happened so quickly.'

Fabian watched the destruction, the mob still scrambling for safety as well as the fire that tore through the arena without mercy.

'Magic,' replied the prince to his lover, as though this word held the answer.

Justas Marl caught the attention of the two young men as they looked around. The other mages, including Tweak, ran out to meet their companions.

'Okay, that's far enough,' Cougar Chuko interjected, holding up a loaded pistol. His troops had joined him and moved swiftly to surround the mages. Marl rolled his eyes. There was very little time for this.

'Do I bore you?' asked Chuko, sounding somewhat peeved.

'You have no idea,' answered Tweak, making a yawning sound on purpose.

'Well, you won't be bored for long. First, I'm going to shoot you, all of you. And then I'm going to—'

'Oh, gods! Someone shut him up!' Marl requested.

'Open fire!'

Those words, rapidly, sent chills down Tweak's spine as he covered his eyes in fear.

Collectively, Cougar's troops started pulling back on their triggers. Nothing happened. Cougar stared, bemused, as did each of his men.

The Cougar aimed and attempted to discharge his own weapon at the mages. Still, nothing happened.

With his acute sense of smell, the Head Hunter sniffed the air and detected the faint sent of gas. It was a sweet, though sickly smell, usually indicative of a certain type of byproduct that ran through the conduits of Urbancloud. A pipe must have ruptured.

The gas is interfering with the gun's triggering mechanisms, The Cougar thought.

'Let's get out of here!' The cowardly creature shouted to his troops.

Katt watched the last poor insignificant wretch flee from the burning arena, his posterior alight which cheered Katt up no end.

'Retreat!' Cougar shouted.

It was time for the mages to do the same.

'Let's go!' Centorionn said, striding off in the direction of the armoury.

'Wait!' Tør told them.

The mages stopped.

'We don't have much time. We have to get back to Mundor immediately,' Marl interjected, hurriedly.

'What is it, Tør?' Fabian turned to the ambassador.

'Since I have been here—since I have been prisoner to these Head Hunters, I have had these strange feelings come over me. It's hard to explain, but I think there are others here too who are trying dearly to escape like us.'

'Who?' asked Fabian, concerned.

'Not who, but what.' Came the reply.

The mages looked at the ambassador with concern and then regarded each other with question.

'It was a feeling in my head—a cry for help.'

'Could you lead us in the direction of this "cry for help"?' asked Marl.

'I might,' the ambassador answered. 'I think we better leave this arena first.'

Marl agreed. The outer circle of tiered seats was already consumed by the blaze.

The mages made their escape through the gladiator's entrance, through the armory and back, via a network of passages, to the detention wing.

The ambassador stopped dead in his tracks. He sat down upon the ground. Like with meditation, his features were serene.

'I shall attempt to make another connection,' he said as the others looked at each other questioningly. 'This is where I first heard the voices. They were loud. Painful to hear. But I shall attempt to hear them again.'

A moment or two went by. There was nothing. The

mind of the ambassador reached outwards to those who had recently contacted him via telepathy.

Marl was growing more and more impatient.

'Come now,' he said, 'we really must make haste.'

The young prince did not answer and walked over to where the ambassador was kneeling.

'Wait,' said the ambassador at last. 'I hear them. They call to me.'

Rising to his feet, Tør sprinted over to the exit. The others followed him. Down a long corridor and a further flight of steps, Tør led the mages to a wide open area.

The ambassador stopped dead, looking left, then right.

'Where now?' asked Fabian.

'There.' The ambassador pointed. At the furthest end of the promenade was a door. It was a large metal door, very thick, and extremely secure.

Marl walked up to the door. There was a panel at the side with a series of buttons all depicting various numerals. A combination lock.

'This will be tricky,' Marl said. 'Now what?'

'Stand aside.' It was Tweak who gave the order.

Marl looked. He shifted his weight quickly to dodge the fine beam of energy as it streaked headlong into the wall panel. What remained of the wall sparked and sizzled from the resulting blast.

The door slid upward quickly, leaving the way clear for the mages to enter.

'Whoa!' Marl made the sound. He looked at the wall and then regarded the dwarf with what appeared to be smoking laser pistol in his hands.

'Tweak?' Fabian said. 'Where did you find that? I thought none of the guns were working.'

'This one does,' said the dwarf.

Beyond the wide open doorway lay the room with the seven orbs.

'What are they?' Iron May asked, only beginning to grasp the significance of the auras that shone like the dual suns of Mundor.

Colonel Warclaw also queried the identities of these orbs. Marl had the faintest inkling, though it was Tweak who recognised the magic that emanated from these seven orbs.

'They are the Skylantern Dragons of old,' the dwarf replied. 'They existed before pre-recorded time, before the great cataclysm. Only snippets of data remain, bits of text, nothing more, and they tell of seven dragons that were once powerful. They were captured by beings even more powerful than they and were stored in a prison of light. This is their light, these are the last remnants of their kind.'

'Yes.' Marl looked at the orbs with wonderment. 'You are right. These are the Skylantern Dragons of legend. But why here? Why now?'

Tweak wandered closer to one of the orbs and was instantly overwhelmed by images of a history long buried. He witnessed the first capture of the Skylantern Dragons and the technology that held them prisoner. He looked on as the dragons showed him the truth. In his mind's eye, Tweak saw everything that had happened, the whole thing, the iniquity and sadness, the burden of being trapped in an orb for so long, and to have greedy, grasping Head Hunters profiteering on such misery.

'How do we free them?' Marl asked.

'With a touch,' Tør answered, closing his eyes. He allowed the prisoners of the orbs to speak to him, to instruct him how to proceed.

His brow wrinkled as he opened his eyes again, turning his questioning gaze to Fabian.

'They want you to free them. They tell me, only you, Fabian, can set them free.'

Fabian's eyes widened with amazement.

'They say only you can unlock the orbs with a

touch. I don't understand why they would request you personally, but they tell me you are the one.'

Fabian looked at the nearest orb. He then looked across at Marl. The mage nodded back as if offering his full blessing.

Uneasily, Fabian reached outwards and pressed his hand against the glowing orb of light. With a brilliant flash of radiance a creature stood where the orb once was. The prison had shattered. It was a large, majestic animal. A dragon! The other orbs flashed and pulsed. They were replaced with dragons too.

'Destiny is on our side,' Marl said.

Back amidst the clouds, the mages rode to safety upon the backs of each respective Skylantern Dragon. They were large, majestic and magic personified. Like Chinese dragons with serpentine forms, they snaked and sailed the winds as destiny had foretold.

Draethor, that man of stone, witnessed the sight as his friends emerge from the great city in the sky, and found himself speechless with awe and admiration. He felt like a soldier again and full of energy for the battle ahead. He witnessed Marl and Fabian both, riders of the Skylantern Dragons, these creatures of myth and legend.

Chapter 13

Twilight, the day's diurnal cycle had given rise to the fear of night's power incarnate. Evil marched upon Mundor and King René knew the end had come. The Monsters of Mundor they had been dubbed. The Sinistrom hordes, armed atop their maggots the size of horses and fuelled by vengeance, recognised that they outnumbered their foes sixteen to one.

Malecarjan, resplendent and confident in his role as warmonger, had secured his dream at last and was soon not only to be master of Mundor, but also to overthrow his betters in a final coup d'état. Even the powerful and mysterious enigma, with his red eyes, his pressed suit, and business demeanour, did not wish to stand in the way of a war. Not this time. This time the order had been given: bring down the enemy's defences!

This delicious subterfuge had been carried out flawlessly. But this was not a war. This was extermination. Even Malecarjan had to concede that a war had to be between two equal powers to necessitate a fair, even conflict; otherwise it was merely a pointless show of force. Mundor was nothing more than an ant beneath the heel.

The Skylantern Dragons, thankful that the mages had freed them from their imprisonment, sailed the skies towards Mundor with the heroes on their backs.

'Look!' The ambassador pointed. Fabian could see the vast armies facing Mundor as they approached. 'It's the Mecha Villeforms! They are marching on Mundor!'

'Not if I have anything to say about it!' replied Prince Fabian, steering his dragon towards a steep embankment.

Malecarjan turned and witnessed the seven specks in the sky, a glint of gold…This was evidence enough that a formidable enemy was approaching. Dragons! Seven of them!

Malecarjan, with a quick turn and swirl of his cloak, leapt atop his winged charger. The saddled creature was a black crow, though it was the size of a barn. It extended wings of plush obsidian. Its master gave it the order to ascend and ascend it did, offering the most chilling sound as it rose higher into the ether.

'Skylantern Dragons,' the zealous warlord muttered with contempt. 'Their power now belongs to the mages of old. Seven dragons for seven mages! This could tip the balance of power in this war. Cougar Chuko will pay dearly for allowing this to happen!'

Malecarjan's mighty steed beat its wings and began to lift high into the stratosphere. The enigma stepped back as the gust from the wings of the beast almost sent him flying backwards. His eyes, blood red, narrowed with contempt for his general. Malecarjan was never good at holding fast. *The impulsive lout*, he thought. With a swift gesture, the enigma ordered the hordes of Mecha Villeforms to start the attack on the kingdom.

The riders went in first atop their equine maggots. First, they chewed at the wooded accesses with their biting beaks, splintering the gates and damaging the beams that had been placed there as buttresses. Soldier's posted upon the battlements shot arrows at the riders. Some of the maggots were killed or subdued in tandem, only to be replaced by another wave, and another.

Eventually, boiling oil was tipped from the battlements, raining down ruin on the hordes below.

King René stood with his men atop the parapets and saw his second and third legions riding over the hill from the north.

The world was a whirlwind of colour, disorientating, frantic like a kaleidoscopic rush—then stillness, shape and contour, sand and sky; there was a sobering stillness, reasserted like a fantastic vision. René watched the black line on the horizon. A shimmering blur stroked the distant dunes. Flanked on his left as he turned his head was a similar sight. On both sides, there was a roar of voices, clear, aggressive. A chilling war cry reverberated through the wasteland.

Two opposing armies on either side populated the horizon, vast enough to consume and obliterate anything caught in the middle. On the one side were the humans, René's warriors, the fighters, generals, and militia, the defence forces. On the other, there was positioned the extraordinary warriors of myth and legend, the harpies, the gorgons, and the fighting centaurs. These were creatures collected from the twelve realms to bolster Kardas' armies. Banners and pennons flourished like waving omens. Behind the front lines, the Titans, taller than mighty elephants, raged with fists and murderous gazes as the armies of man drew nearer. Upon dinosaurs, they rode, beasts like the triceratops and the brachiosaur. They had mighty arrows, these titans, arrows the size of trees, tapered at one end, feathered at the other, which they shot from bows the size of houses. These mythic creatures had magnitude and brute strength on their side. They could strike panic into the men who feared only what they could not understand. Yes, and poor René looked this way and then that, unable to utter a sound.

Each opposing side marched on the other. There were the Naegorns, the two-headed creatures with the top half of their bodies all covered in fur and the lower half sheltered with fish scales. In addition, there were the Magnoperes, half-human, harpy-like with webbed wings and monstrous talons that could rend steel with a single deadly strike.

One side appeared more formidable than the other. The humans opened up with everything they had. Some of the mythic creatures were cut down by the first volley, while others, who were more resilient, managed to cut through the lines. Blood was drawn. A huge Saebormorph, a creature whose skin exuded knives, rushed at his human enemies, impaling one after another.

The king watched in silence as a fifteen-foot Titan bounded into the tussle and began swinging a giant mace that in turn levelled the playing field—bodies were sent pitching in all directions.

The Minotaurs were more concerned for their

appetites than they were for the war effort. They sat and devoured their human victims, rediscovering the taste for blood, a flavour their ancestors knew well. The Gorgons in the interim took down their enemy with a single look, converting every human into stone.

It was a slaughter. The Centaurs sounded the cavalry with their giant horns. Mighty winged harpies descended upon men and carried them off into the stratosphere where oxygen was scarce. Basilisks slithered round the fray of feet, selecting their prey one at a time. Men would look into the blood-red eyes of the basilisks and fall dead instantly without being touched or physically maimed.

The human race was losing.

The cries of those who were dying continued to resound around the falling kingdom. A man who was injured lay suffering a metre from where another soldier knelt, blood oozing from every cut.

'Help me,' he seemed to say in a faltering voice. The other soldier watched feebly as a titan picked the injured man up and held him fast in his powerful arms.

King René felt his heart falter, fearing what was about to come at last. Nothing could save him or his people. At that precise moment he knew what he had to do: he would cast his own body from the battlements and hurl his remains down into the waters of the moat far below. Failure could demand nothing more. In his final moment he looked up and noticed something which he could barely make out at first. Then, as the specks in the distance came ever nearer, he saw…

The mages witnessed the approaching crow and broke formation, allowing Malecarjan to pass between them. Justas Marl banked to the left, his dragon had a vested interest in Malecarjan, he noticed. He didn't even have to command his mount. His airborne steed had a will of its own: that will was bent on revenge. The dragon was gaining, steam billowing in plumes of smoke. The devil was in its gaze. This was understandable since it was Malecarjan who had stolen some of the dragon's powers back at Urban Cloud. Now the creature wanted retribution.

'I know that dragon,' Malecarjan growled, opening the palm of his hand to allow the magic he had stolen to generate like a bright, glowing nucleus. He forged a mighty orb of energy, focusing it in his palm, and then hurled it right at the Skylantern Dragon.

Justas Marl commanded his dragon: 'Dive! Dive now!'

His dragon was in control and dived out of the way

just as the magic thunderbolt passed them. The dragon breathed in and, positioning itself to attack, spat fire at the enemy. The crow reared, losing a number of its dark feathers.

Malecarjan turned his head to look behind. The Skylantern Dragon was on his tail. The crow pitched and plummeted. The dragon followed. Malecarjan dazzled his pursuers with a burst of magic which he summoned again. He used this dragon's power against it, blinding it temporarily. Then the black crow rose again to a safe altitude. The blinded dragon hit, sending Marl hurtling to the ground.

Laughing, the wicked Malecarjan rose higher and higher, free to rejoin the rest of his hordes.

The other mages alighted right in the thick of battle. Their Skylanterns forced the armies back with the fire of their breath.

Draethor, the man of stone, raised a giant slab of granite above his head and hurled it at the Sinistrom. The result was a clump of mashed maggots and their riders, which triggered a glowing smile on Draethor's flinty face.

The Sinistrom forces retaliated, but figured they were no match for the stone fists that had taken a wallop at one enemy and sent others fleeing in abject fear. In the thick of it, Colonel Warclaw transformed himself into a colossal crab and started picking off the Sinistrom one by one.

'This is getting out of hand,' the ambassador said, seated behind Fabian. The dragon persisted to carry the prince and the ambassador on its great back. It reared its head to look behind suddenly and witnessed the black shape in the distance, that fowl, distinct shape, Malecarjan's crow-like carrier, and it was clearly poised for another attack.

'Come dragon!' The prince requested the legendary creature. 'Drop us off over there!'

Fabian steered his dragon closer to the ground, allowing the ambassador to jump and land safely on terra firma.

'That is enough!' Tør cried.

John Dafoe, the man who had been ordered merely to oversee the war, turned instantly on his heels. His red eyes enlarged, incapable of believing the vision that approached him. *Could this be the ambassador?* he thought.

Tør, once he was in earshot, offered a clear directive to his father's associate:

'Stop this instant! King René was not responsible for my kidnapping!'

John saw his liege heading towards him. Admittedly, he was surprised to see the boy was still alive.

'Ambassador, my liege!' John said, bending down on one knee.

'What happened? How did you…?'

'I don't know,' Tør replied in all honesty. 'I did not recognise my captors, but they were not of Mundor, I can promise you that. In fact, it was Prince Fabian here who rescued me.'

The prince jumped down from his dragon and approached the two.

'I see,' John said, thoughtfully. 'But by all eye witness accounts you were abducted by a dragon, and here we have six mages, a prince of Mundor, and all here in the service of King René, commanding seven dragons in battle. Now, I have to admit, this is not a coincidence. Dragons on this world have been near extinct for what…centuries? A couple of millennia? Really? There can't be that many people around who own a dragon, much less command one.'

John cast Tør Vallor a look that bordered on the humiliatingly pitiful.

Tør drew a breath to state what he believed was the truth, and a greave injustice.

'They really did save me! These brave men. This bold young man came to save me from my captors.'

The man lowered his red-tinged eyes introspectively and then looked at Fabian, at once appearing to lose the hardness of his features.

Tør witnessed the sudden thoughtfulness upon John's face. He saw this as an opportunity to speak further:

'Fabian's people are innocent.'

John turned on his heels.

Behind the battle, the horn blower, a solitary Sinistrom soldier, watched his commanding officer approach him.

'Sound the horn,' the enigma said to him. 'Tell the troops to stand down immediately.'

As the horn blower began to press his lips against the mouth piece.

'No!' came a cry, suddenly.

John was almost knocked off his feet as an immense black shadow passed over him. The stygian riding crow halted in the smoke-laden ether. It remained, hovering, beating its colossal wingspan, generating a mighty current of air. A figure shifted position in the saddle, strapped to the great bird's back, and jumped clear of the mount, landing just a few feet away from John's position.

'You will not stop this battle!' Malecarjan threatened, taking measurable strides towards John's position. 'Malecarjan!' He shouted. 'What is the meaning of this?'

Malecarjan did not answer. He drew his weapon to cut his commanding officer down in cold blood.

Quickly, John acted. He raised his right hand in a defensive gesture. This began to repel his attacker.

Malecarjan felt a powerful force pushing him back. He weathered it. He called upon the power of the Skylantern Dragon, the power that was given to him by the Head Hunter at Urban Cloud. His hands began to glow. The two bright orbs that shone through the darkness of his visor grew brighter as they discharged a mighty surge of power.

'You will die!'

John felt the power of the discharge hit him full on in the chest. He fell to his knees. The onslaught was enough to fully subdue him. John was floored in a moment's breath.

Again, the horn blower pressed his lips against the mouthpiece.

In the distance, a catapult fired a rock at the battlements.

Malecarjan, using his new dragon powers, forced the projectile to change its trajectory. He sent in the direction of the horn blower, crushing the man under its considerable weight.

The battle continued.

Malecarjan rejoined his mount, taking flight above the horror and the bloodshed.

The Ambassador stood there, speechless. The whole senseless horror of it had not fully sunk in. Fabian, realising all was probably not lost yet, placed his hand on his lover's shoulder.

'Come on! There's nothing we can do for them! Come on, we have to go!'

Fabian took him by the hand and guided him to the dragon that was waiting for them. They mounted the great beast. In no time at all, they were airborne again.

King René was still up on the battlements. His men had successfully repelled an attempt by the enemy to reach the higher walls using wooden ladders. He watched with amazement as, upon the distant wall, a dragon had docked, letting off two passengers, the Sinistrom Ambassador and the prince.

'What does that boy think he's doing?' the king raged, drawing his sword and running in the direction of the two young people.

Malecarjan turned his head, looking down upon the battlements as the king ran towards his son and the ambassador.

The black clad knight ordered his flying steed to take wing near the ramparts between father and son. The giant crow did as its master commanded. Before long, Malecarjan was soaring over the parapets. Bowmen were firing their arrows to try and repel the invader. Malecarjan jumped from his mount, drawing his sword as he freefell and landed squarely upon the wall, slaughtering as many armed parties that presented themselves.

King René, seeing the obstacle that stood betwixt him and his son, stopped dead in his tracks. Malecarjan stood still, his back arched, his head low, turned to view the king of Mundor. Eyes burned like a sizzling furnace behind the shield grating of his helmet. His sword, freshly bloodied, was drawn from the gizzard of a victim. Sadly, not the last either. The cruel warmonger turned his head and then rose to full stature. He commenced to stride along the battlements, his confidence unmatched. He walked towards the king. René prepared his sword to repel the trespasser. Malecarjan stood at least a couple of feet taller than his adversary, though René had seen off a number of giants in his day. He was unafraid.

He swung his sword, though missed. The dark-clad knight knocked the potentate backwards with a burst of magic that surged from his black gauntlet.

'No!' shouted Fabian, running to protect his father. In mid dash he metamorphosed before the invader's eyes. Human muscle and sinew was quickly replaced by reptilian power and strength. The neck elongated to sprout the fanged head and red eyes. The hands and feet became larger and clawed. The giant webbed wings developed as well, sprouting from his back like violent sepals.

Malecarjan summoned what was left of the magic he had stolen from the Skylantern and used it to quell the Dragon Tolan. Fabian was thrust backwards by an energy barrier which knocked him out for a brief time.

The ambassador, who had never witnessed Fabian's transformation before, watched but could barely believe. Fabian was the Dragon Tolan? He was indeed the creature that had plucked him from the market square, only to kidnap him and use him to start this horrific war!

The shadowy knight turned back to the king who had barely begun to pick himself up after his last attack.

'Proof enough,' Malecarjan said, pointing to the Dragon Tolan laying unconscious, 'is it not? Your son and that creature, both one and the same, and you conspired to kidnap our liege.'

Malecarjan poised before the king of Mundor and motioned towards the prince, the Dragon Tolan, on the floor.

'This boy dragon,' he began, 'this mutation, abortion, started your war, King René! You fathered a monster, and, like all monsters, he has no awareness of right or wrong, no ethical, moral fibre. As such, he saw fit to start this war by extravagant and nefarious means. Obviously, the apple fell slightly further from the tree, as I gather, since you, King René, would have been loutish enough simply to draw first blood, literally speaking of course.'

'How dare you!' The king raged, clambering to his feet at last. As Fabian transformed back into a boy, finding consciousness again, he looked on as Malecarjan seized the king by his throat. The monster hoisted him up, choking and sputtering. René's hands desperately tried to loosen his attacker's superhuman grip.

'You, René. You are the one who sat by and let your degenerate son kidnap the ambassador. I ought to choke you here and now. But I believe in poetic justice. You who tend to dragons. You who fathered a dragon. You will learn the true power of the dragon.'

Malecarjan hurled the man a distance.

'This is your punishment, your highness!'

King René landed a few meters away, clutching at his throat and choking, gasping for air. Fabian looked at his father, kneeling. He had just had the wind knocked out of him. Fabian then regarded the monster that stood between them, his back facing him. Malecarjan did not notice the prince as he ran to join his father, though noticed quickly the approaching footfalls and did nothing to hinder the son and heir as he darted passed him.

'Father!' he called out.

Malecarjan summoned the last ounce of power and sent a blast hurtling towards the ground where King René lay. Fabian dived suddenly, holding his hand out in a bid to save his father from falling to his death. The stone crumbled and collapsed beneath the king's feet. Fabian managed to clasp the man's hand just as he was about to plunge.

The warmonger leapt upon his riding crow and soared into the sky, cackling stridently as he watched his handiwork.

King René knew his end had come with the dishonour which had been laid at his feet by his only son.

'You degenerate bastard!' René spat poison back at Fabian as he dangled hundreds of feet above the lower levels of the castle. 'I should have killed you when you were a child. Monster, let go of me! Let me fall!'

The king flailed about as he spoke.

Fabian felt the strain on his arm. Tears of stress and pain began to pour down his face as the man, his father, suspended above a death-dealing height, began to squeeze his hand tightly, allowing the increasing pressure to hurt his son. Fabian recalled just how tightly his father could grip another's hand. The boy gritted his teeth as the pain shot up his arm suddenly.

'Father! Stop it now! I want to save you! Give me your other hand! Please! I did not betray you! Please, let me pull you up!'

'No! I am dishonoured, and I am ashamed to have you as my son. I would sooner die than live another second on this dark day.'

The pain of his father's crushing grip mixed with the agony of his words was truly too much for the prince to bear.

'It was a lie!' The boy went on explaining. 'Malecarjan lied. I didn't betray you! I was set up!'

At that moment, Fabian lost his grip. He felt his father's hand slip through his fingers. The transformation came suddenly. In the boy's place, the Dragon Tolan had the added reach and strength to save the king from falling.

An explosion shook the ground under which the dragon knelt. The king's arm slipped from the creature's grip. The man fell to his death.

Dragon Tolan eyes, filled with terror and sadness, changed back to familiar human orbits. Fabian shouted after him, the sound that stuck in the ambassador's ears, the chords of which strummed at his heartstrings like a desolate player.

Tør went over to Fabian and held him close in his arms. The prince kicked and yelled and suffered greatly over the sudden loss. A massive blast took half the battlements in a deafening explosion of fire. The wall shook, and Fabian looked up at the sky, blood-red with the conflagrations of battle.

Rising slowly to his feet, the prince felt the heat of anger poach within the centres of his mind and his eyes. Yes, he rose. He mounted the upper battlements and looked down upon the frenzy of battle below.

Tør rose also as he watched, concerned that grief would take his friend and hurl his poor, misunderstood life down into the ditch of death that lay before him.

He called his name. It was far too late.

Fabian stood up and, taking one look at his father's doomed kingdom, decided finally to allow vengeance to consume him. He stepped up onto the ramparts and hurled himself off of them, his lover screaming behind him.

The Dragon Tolan once again showed itself, splaying its wings apart as it circled the battlefield.

Tør ran to the spot and stared over the edge.

It came as a relief to witness the Tolan, Fabian's strange though magnificent alter ego as it rose higher and higher, only to dive, casting its body over the unsuspecting hordes of the Sinistrom below.

Some of the Skylantern Dragons merged in formation with Fabian.

The mages in the meantime looked up at that glorious moment as the reptiles in collusion rushed over them, sending up a great draft of air that brought many of the Sinistrom hurtling off their feet. The other mages sought cover amidst the hollows as the Mecha Villeforms and their monstrous allies stood mesmerised. There was merely a second's calm as the dragons in formation moved back round for another pass, this time opening up with everything they had, scorching the battlefield with the hottest fire known to man: dragon fire!

Maggot riders were reduced to bone as the flesh was melted from their bodies. One Titan drew his weapon to take out a Skylantern only to have his head bitten clean off by one of them taking up the rear. Its red eyes rolled back as it devoured the giant, followed by another that swallowed the rest of the arms, legs, feet, the lot.

Malecarjan, realising that the war was lost, fled for the horizon atop his giant crow mount. His desire for blood was sated in any case.

In the blood-red mist, Marl woke with a sudden start. His dragon mount also came to with a deafening roar. The other viper masters were scurrying into the trees. Ophidia departed with her battalion of snake warriors, scurrying off into the dense forest that flanked the kingdom.

The shapeshifter, Tai Pan, who had been watching from behind the lines all this time, transformed himself into the Dragon Tolan, mimicking Fabian's alter ego once more. This time he would use this form, not to discredit his victims, but to escape reprisal.

The false Dragon Tolan rose high into the air.

Tør witnessed the sudden emergence as he sat atop the battlements. He saw the wings extend from tip to tip. The Dragon Tolan that was an exact copy flew overhead, causing loose stonework to crumble to the floors below. Yet the true Dragon Tolan, Fabian was circling the battlefield. What trickery was this? Could there have been a second Dragon Tolan?

Chapter 14

Much of the kingdom of Mundor would have to be rebuilt. But no one could reconstitute the lives that had been ruined or lost in this fruitless war. The ancients would have called it a pyrrhic victory.

Fabian returned to human form and gravely went about assessing the destruction. Justas Marl, Tweak, and the ambassador accompanied him as he explored the rooms of the palace, the gardens, and the marketplace and shops. In the souk where they stood rubble covered the cobbled streets, leaving only twisted metal and holes where shops and houses once resided.

'We can help rebuild,' Marl offered, placing a hand on the boy's shoulder.

'Thank you,' said the boy, sombrely.

Marl waited a moment before saying:

'Your advisors would like to talk to you about a certain matter. There is a vacuum of power which will need to be filled and…'

'Not now, Marl, please.' Fabian warned with a certain amount of sharpness.

'Of course.' Marl granted, realising his place.

'Now is not the time.' The ambassador continued, holding Fabian's hand. They both walked away to enjoy one another's company alone.

'I was wrong to have judged that boy.' Tweak mentioned with certain regret, watching the two youths walk out of earshot.

Justas Marl placed a reassuring hand on the dwarf's shoulder.

'Don't be too hard on yourself. I believe you have learned a valued lesson, my friend. We know there are tempests capable of turning father against son, and neighbour against neighbour. In time, Mundor will be rebuilt. On that day this kingdom will be stronger and much more prepared for that storm on the skyline. I fear though that the emotional scars may linger.'

In the part of that arboretum left untainted, the section that had left its mark upon the two lovers since the first night they met, Fabian and the ambassador remained together watching the moon appear in the sky.

'It is where we began,' the ambassador said.

Fabian was understandably silent.

Tør noted the distance in Fabian's eyes.

'It must have been hard on you...keeping this secret. The years spent guarding it like a discomforting ailment...or curse.'

Fabian smiled ironically.

'The worst part is...he will never know. My father passed away without ever having realised the strengths I had. My failings as a son bloomed from what he failed to perceive were his own failings as a father.'

The prince turned to face Tør.

'It is because I was so terrified of my alter ego, I was scared that people would fear me and make me an outcast. Somehow, even when I wasn't aware of the dragon's presence I felt it: a monster living inside me.'

'Not a monster...' said the ambassador suddenly. 'When I saw your Tolan fight in the arena on Urban Cloud I had no idea it was you. And when I saw you endeavour to stop the war, and for the first time you transformed into the great fiery Tolan, I did not quite know what to think. But I did see you. Or rather I saw another, identical Tolan Dragon. I saw the other fly overhead, escaping the scene. And I wondered, how could there be two Tolans? How was that possible? But I knew then the question was irrelevant. I knew, it wasn't you. It wasn't you!'

He lifted Fabian's chin.

'You are not a monster, Fabian. You're a good soul.'

Fabian smiled as a solitary tear trickled down his cheek.

Days and weeks passed and a date for the coronation was decided. Much of the royal palace was still under heavy reconstruction. But the halls and rooms were free of the clutter and rubble at last. Pennons were raised, and the courts were once again filled with the shouts of joyful people.

Fabian sat upon his throne as the page mounted the diadem upon his youthful head. Tweak smiled a big jolly smile and the people cheered and clapped.

In the square one elderly woman said to another:

'He's more handsome than his father.'

'Oh, yes, I know.' The other agreed. 'I think he'll make a grand king.'

Later, as the sun faded over the western hill, Justas Marl knocked at the king's bedchamber door.

'Enter!' Came the familiar voice within.

Marl opened the door and crossed the threshold. Colonel Warclaw and Iron May were with him.

King Fabian rose from his armchair. He had been

looking out over his veranda at the setting sun, thinking about recent events.

'Pardon this intrusion, my liege.'

The two mages bowed in respect.

'There's no need to apologise,' the king said. 'Please, rise. Tell me; to what do I owe the honour of this visit?'

'My liege, we were leaving and would just like to convey our sincerest thanks for the time we have spent here.'

'Come on.' Fabian smiled, dropping the act. 'You don't have to stand on ceremony, not round me. We've all been through a lot together, and it should be I thanking you for all that you've done for me and my people. Without you, I would not have been able to come to terms with my other self, and I would not have found my true friends, the Skylantern Dragons and, consequently, without you, I would not have been able to salvage my kingdom.'

'Well, remember, you are the seventh mage.' Marl reminded promptly. 'You are our brother. And I would be proud to have you with us one more time for another adventure.'

Tears started to flow.

'Brother? No...no.' The king corrected, his voice beginning to crack under the pressure of his emotions.

'I would proffer to call you Father. My own biological father called me monster, and never understood me, or acknowledged me except to bring shame to my existence. You are my father, Marl. You who taught and nurtured me both as Fabian and as the dragon within me. Tolan means warrior in the language of my people. And I wish to thank you for making me realise that I have a fighter's heart, and a noble spirit within me.'

The two moved closer to each other and hugged. It had been a very long time since he had felt this complete in his life, and he was sorry when the mages had to leave finally. But they promised they would return within the year and they would spend more time together.

Katt Brutal remained outside. She lay in the shade, dreamily remembering her recent adventures. Unexpectedly, she caught the scent of something vaguely familiar in the air.

Waking, she caught a sudden flash of something in the sky above her. *It is too large to be a bird*, she thought. Whatever it was, it alighted and settled upon the verdant lawn in front of her. She sat up suddenly, catching the winged creature's eye. It was a baby dragon, the only one of its kind. No doubt it had recently been spawned by one of the freed Skylanterns. It made a yawning sound.

It was so cute, the way it sat there with its mouth gaping wide open.

Katt suddenly darted off to tell the others, crying excitedly, 'It's a child! It's a child!'

The others came to see what all the commotion was.

Full of curiosity, Marl came to the instant conclusion that this was indeed a child of the Skylantern Dragons. Its many tiny scales that adorned it like a dazzling Koi Carp were the brightest gold. The horns on the back of its head, which were small and undeveloped, would one day grow and curl to form types of antlers capable of wreaking damage upon wrong-doers and ne'er-do-wells.

'Is it dangerous?' Tweak asked, hiding behind the legs of his king and only taking a peak around the corner gingerly, in cowardly fashion, to see if the coast was clear.

'It is quite safe.' Marl asserted as he bent down to pick the infant creature up.

'A pet for the king.' He suggested.

'But is it house broken?' asked King Fabian, taking a step forwards.

At that precise moment the dragon leapt from Marl's hands to land squarely in the arms of the king. The potentate flinched as a massive, wet, forked tongue slid mercilessly along his face. Not wanting another barrage of licks – though not wishing to offend the creature since all he was offering was his affection really – Fabian held the dragon further away, though with a gentle will for refusal, at arm's length.

'I think he's house broken.' Iron May observed dryly.

'I think its love,' the dwarf muttered to himself.

'Perhaps you and Tør can adopt' Katt joked. 'Under Sinistrom rule, I think it would be allowed.'

Fabian tightened his lips as the others laughed. Though the happy banter was not lost on Fabian, and he joined in with the high spirits.

That same day the treaty was signed.

'Today marks the beginning of a new era for us!' Fabian exclaimed from behind his podium. The people cheered. As the applauding slowly faded Fabian said, 'We can live free! Safe! We can look to the future and know peace and security in our souls! We are free!'

As Fabian turned he caught the smile on Tør's face.

The sounds of support from the crowd seemed almost deafening.

Tør folded the signed accords and placed them in his portfolio. Then he too started to clap and cheer.

'The future! Long live the king! Long live king Fabian!'

Thank you for taking the time to read Skylantern Dragons and the Monsters of Mundor. If you enjoyed it, please consider telling your friends or posting a short review on Amazon. Word of mouth is very valuable and would be very much appreciated. Thank you.

Scott William Taylor